BEATRICE AIRD O'HANLON h
novels, *Return to Coolavella* and C
Beatrice is a nurse/midwife wi
Classical Civilsation, TCD, 1984. S.
worked for many years in clinical research.
Beatrice lives with her husband Michael in Delgany.

THE TREACLE SEA

AND OTHER STORIES

by Beatrice Aird O'Hanlon
Illustrated by Jane Langwall

SilverWood

Published in 2018 by SilverWood Books

SilverWood Books Ltd
14 Small Street, Bristol, BS1 1DE, United Kingdom
www.silverwoodbooks.co.uk

ISBN 978-1-78132-750-0

British Library Cataloguing in Publication Data
A CIP catalogue record for this book is available from the British Library

Page design and typesetting by SilverWood Books
Printed on responsibly sourced paper

Contents

The Treacle Sea

Out in the wide blue ocean, a family of marine friends made their home in an old shipwreck. The King of Spain had dispatched the ship hundreds of years ago to wage war on the high seas.

The ship broke up amid the perilous storms that raged around the jagged coasts. The jutting rocks ripped the keel from the boat, scattering its priceless possessions all over the seabed. It was now a perfect home for small marine creatures.

There it lay, a splendid ship, at the bottom of the ocean. The huge abandoned wreck, built of the finest oak wood, was laden with gold and silver coins and wondrous objects. Inside its great belly lay an enormous upturned marble table, and around it delicate porcelain and glassware were scattered. It had lain there undisturbed in the timelessness of the ocean. Golden goblets and silver candlesticks were strewn everywhere on the ocean bed. Caskets filled with priceless sapphires and emeralds remained embedded in the seabed. Exotic animals made from precious gold and studded with rubies had been stuck in the sand for hundreds of years.

Creatures clambered over and inside heavy bronze cauldrons; others slept among jewelled swords, daggers and cutlasses, and in suits of armour. Some creatures propelled themselves along the ship's enormous mast, now home to long swirling tails of seaweed and dotted with clinging shellfish. Then there were those who made their homes inside the huge bronze cannons that once raged war and fired gunpowder for miles across the great oceans.

There was Henrietta Herring, who hated being part of a large shoal of fish and much preferred to cross the waters on her own, seeking out all kinds of interesting gullies and crevices in the varied ocean bed. Henrietta was in her prime, a young silver herring who darted and moved her elegant fins with grace among the waters. She loved to glide inside the dark belly of a massive cannon to find out who had moved in and who was still clinging to its great rusty body.

There was Mabel, a large greedy, selfish crab who slept in a treasure chest, nesting herself among priceless gold and silver sovereigns and resting her claws on jewels that shimmered in the waters. Golden coins and doubloons crinkled around the chest.

Each night, as Mabel slept on her treasures, she thought that she was the luckiest crab in the entire seabed, as no other creature had a bed so delightful with so many interesting shapes and objects that shimmered and shone.

Olivia was a carefree lobster who liked nothing more than exploring all the inlets that were to be found in this part of the ocean. She made her home in the once proud ship's galley, where the food used to be prepared. Here she had lots of little box-like shapes into which she crept and scuttled around. It made a perfect home for the curious lobster. But when she was really tired, Olivia liked nothing more than to stretch her weary limbs on a great round golden plate, studded with diamonds, which had been used to deliver secret and important notes to the captain of this great vessel.

Hundreds of marine creatures all clung, thrived and made their home on this mighty wreck.

Then disaster struck. One moment the sun's rays came through the ocean, the next everything went dark; thick and black like treacle. The sea creatures were barely able to see anything around them. A huge oil tanker had struck the jagged and perilous rocks and spilled hundreds of tonnes of crude oil all over the sea. A layer of treacle-like slick covered this once wild and beautiful area, and all the creatures underneath became cold and gloomy.

Henrietta wondered where all of her friends had gone. Nothing stirred in the dark sea. Surely Mabel or Olivia were around somewhere. She waited in the freezing waters, but all was still and eerily silent. After days searching, she just about made out Olivia, waddling along weakly on her frail legs. She was followed by poor Mabel, who was barely able to lift her large awkward frame on her tottering claws.

Henrietta swam up to greet them.

"Mabel, Olivia, am I glad to find you! Isn't it awful about the oil spill? I can't see anything, and there's precious little to eat!"

Mabel was clearly distraught and without a sparkle in her voice remarked, "Henrietta, there's no food around, the water is disgusting, and we are sick most of the time. All

I can see is a dark cloudy mess in front of me, and I simply can't breathe." With that, she coughed and spluttered to show how much her poor feathery gills, at the top of her legs, had suffered from the recent spillage. The two friends then clambered up and settled on a ledge as they were quite exhausted.

Henrietta was very upset to see how miserable her friends were. She could barely make out their wretched expressions in the dull icy depths. She said, "Look, I've a great idea. What do you say to a plan to move out of here? Let's find a new place where the water is clear and where we can at least breathe again. I heard from some sardines the other day that there are clean seas over by the west. It would involve some travelling, but we would all be together and can look out for each other. They say that it is full of rocks and reefs and interesting bays, as well as the remains of an old church which fell into the sea hundreds of years ago. And you never know, we might just come across another shipwreck where we can settle down again. I hear that the whole place is littered with wrecks."

"You must be mad! That's far away from here. It would take us days to get there," mumbled Mabel, who was quite content to sit it out and become more and more ill rather than move. She hated the thought of some other creature lying among the precious jewels in her treasure chest.

"I agree with Henrietta. We'll just die if we stay here. I had a chat with Garry Gannet today, and he said that he was finding it very difficult to preen his nice silky feathers – they've got all greasy and soggy...and we all know how proud he was of his beautiful plumage," sighed Olivia hobbling off into the nearest crevice, so crestfallen she had become with the lack of light. Olivia was very curious and always ready to take up a challenge, unlike her friend Mabel.

"Who cares what the fellow thinks! We're better off without him and his kind, who just eat all of the best food around anyway, diving from the sky with his beady eyes, the greedy gannet!" mumbled Mabel, to no one in particular.

"Mabel, we hope you change your mind. We'll get ourselves ready and be off the day after tomorrow," Henrietta said and off she swam with her tail flipping back and forth. She was really very excited at the prospect of the move.

Mabel went to bed that night in a terrible state at the thought of leaving her beautiful home on the seabed. She could not settle in her treasure chest as she was so stressed. She woke up the next morning and found herself completely entangled in a sumptuous gold collar set in pearls and rubies, worn by a Spanish nobleman long ago.

"I must have been having my crab nightmares again. Oh dear, it's going to take me ages to unravel myself from all this gold," she said as her sharp teeth bit into a piece of the precious metal.

Near Henrietta's hideout lived some sponges. They were quiet and kept to themselves. They led mostly uneventful lives, just sitting there nodding and waving their awkward shapes in the ocean. They really were hopeless company, thought Henrietta. "Well, I certainly won't miss them. They are very boring really!"

"Hi, Henrietta." Making a swift U-turn with her tail, she spied Orla the scallop wheeling her way towards her. Orla was a pale coloured orange shellfish with pretty designs on her elegant seashell. Her shell was in the shape of a fan, which allowed her to move swiftly in bursts when attacked.

"Orla, I'm always amazed at how you move by sucking water in, between the little spaces in your shell. It's so perfect."

"Oh, I suppose it's one of those things I've always done, just like you swimming and darting with a flick of your tail," gurgled Orla. Orla and her kind were said to have the most elegant shells of all the marine creatures, so much so that the scallop shell had become a symbol of great beauty.

"How are you managing with all this oil? Isn't it dreadful?" whispered Henrietta, darting around the scallop.

"Well, you know how sensitive we scallops are to our surrounds. Most of my friends and family have left or died in the oil-filled sea, but thankfully I'm still here, although all I can see are strange dark movements in the water now," Orla said. Henrietta noticed that Orla seemed anxious, as her hundred beady little sapphire blue eyes darted everywhere.

"Orla, I have a plan. We are thinking of moving out of here, and you're very welcome to join us. Mabel and Olivia will be coming too," Henrietta said gently, knowing that scallops can only move short distances and in spurts.

"No thanks, I'll stay here." Orla had no intention of

accompanying Henrietta, as she knew that Mabel liked nothing better than to munch on a nice juicy scallop. Then she said, "Oops, sorry, I've got to go – here comes that dreadful Stephen again," and with that Orla snapped her shell shut and wheeled her way down to the bottom of the ocean and disappeared. Henrietta spied Stephen Starfish scrambling along the seabed in search of Orla. He then squeezed under a narrow crevice and disappeared.

Betty Barnacle was frantic, searching for a clean surface on the underside of one of the many great metal guns to cling to, and was clearly distracted. Great chunks of the gun metal had rusted with time, clinging creatures and long drapes of seaweed to its surface.

"Hi, Betty. A group of friends and I are going to leave these dark and polluted waters to seek a fresher place to live, so I've come to say goodbye," Henrietta greeted the busy barnacle.

Betty hardly looked at Henrietta as she beat her feathery legs rhythmically to draw in some plankton and try to cling onto her home on the wreck.

"I can barely get enough to eat with this awful oil spill. Oh well, I'll just keep trying. Goodbye, Henrietta, and I wish you the best of luck. I'd love to live somewhere else, but we have to stay put. With all of the children we have, I couldn't possibly move." She began to kick furiously with her legs to draw in more plankton.

Word got around locally that Henrietta, Mabel and Olivia were about to embark on a great adventure. A mature grey mullet fish, called Mike Mullet, met them in the underwater twilight as they were preparing to take their leave of the wreck and introduced himself.

"Is it true that you girls are heading out on a long perilous journey which will take you far away from the wreck? But where will you go?" the mullet fish asked. Henrietta could not believe how unadventurous some marine creatures were.

"To fresher waters, of course. We can't stay here, or we'll die. Why, it's like living in permanent twilight. There's just not enough food for all, now that the seas have been polluted, and if you have any sense at all, you'll move too, as it will take years to clean up this mess." And with that the brave little herring weaved and darted around him.

"And will it be safe travelling in these dark waters?" the mullet ventured to ask, his eyes wide in wonder and curiosity.

"Who knows? That's a chance we'll have to take," Henrietta answered in a low soothing voice.

"It sounds like a great idea. You know, I'm not getting any younger, and I've nothing to lose, and certainly I can't hang around here, so if it's OK with you, I'll tag along too," the mullet said, after giving the adventure some thought.

"That's great, Mike! You and your kind are strong energetic swimmers, so we would be delighted to have you join us," Henrietta said to him, with a flick of her tail.

Some eager sardines and a few friendly jellyfish decided to move as well with their little group.

Having discussed the merits of heading off on this great adventure with Olivia, her best friend, Mabel decided to leave with the group. That night she clambered into her great treasure chest for the last time and fell sound asleep as she dreamt of her journey out in the wide unknown.

The next day the small party set out on their big adventure. Henrietta and Mike Mullet led the way. Henrietta's silver dorsal fin acted like a flag for the party to follow. They

travelled slowly at first until Olivia and Mabel discovered a way to propel themselves along to keep up with the others.

"Please, not so fast! I can't keep up," spluttered poor Mabel as Olivia flicked a sea slug to the tired crab to keep her happy. Henrietta peered behind and could barely make out Mabel's shape in the distance.

"Mabel, please try and move all those feathery bits, and do try and hurry up," Henrietta said. Mabel then made a gallant attempt and with great effort moved all her paddle-shaped limbs to propel herself along.

Olivia's curiosity caused her to stop and to inspect every pool, crevice and gully along the way. She was such an inquisitive creature. She wandered off and became separated from the little group. Soon the rest of the group realised that Olivia was nowhere to be seen. Henrietta was furious at the lobster's carefree attitude.

"Why does Olivia have to be so thoughtless, scuttling off on her own like this instead of staying with the group? She is always poking around pools and holes, searching for really nothing at all. She is so nosy. Why, it's no wonder that some of her family and friends climbed into fishermen's pots and ended up as lobster mayonnaise. Her curiosity will simply lead her into all kinds of danger. Now we'll all be delayed searching for her. We really do need to get going before we get any weaker. Her wanderings will be our downfall," Henrietta spoke to the little group assembled.

They all nodded and agreed that Olivia had been reckless and careless in wandering off on her own and becoming separated from the group. Mabel was upset that she might never see her best friend again. She started to cry, great big blobs of crab tears streaming from her beady little eyes.

"Poor silly Olivia, she's probably struggling in some horrible fisherman's pot with a lot of other crabs and lobsters, with no room to move. I can't even begin to think what she's going through," she sobbed.

Mike Mullet came over and put a comforting fin

around Mabel's ample girth. Like all mullets, he did not like to witness any kind of upset and upheaval. He and his species avoided trouble and always settled where the waters were calm.

"There, there, Mabel, don't upset yourself. Olivia is too clever to end up in a pot. Look, I have an idea. Why don't I go and search for her? I can dart around the place and see if I can find her. She can't have gone too far," he said swimming around and showing off his beautiful blue fins. So Mike Mullet set out to patrol the waters in search of Olivia. They watched as his dark blue shape darted away in the waters in the quest for the little lobster.

Meanwhile they encountered some gossipy sea urchins who kept them up-to-date with the entire goings-on in the seabed.

"Have you seen a nice-looking, curious young lobster, by any chance? She has very distinctive long tentacles for a young female," Henrietta asked them.

They bobbed and made strange little noises among themselves.

"Oh yes, we saw her. Silly little thing – she went scuttling off, peering into depths and crevices. On and on she went, down and down until she was out of sight in the dark waters of the deep and she just disappeared," a cheeky young urchin babbled.

The group remained silent as their worst fears were realised.

"That's it. I'll never see my best friend again," moaned Mabel, and she started sobbing once more with great big crab tears, so that one of the jellyfish had to supply her with some sea ferns to wipe her eyes.

Meanwhile Mike Mullet glided and searched the waters. He was soon exhausted looking for Olivia. But sadly he searched in vain. The curious lobster was nowhere to be found. On and on he ventured, darting among the holes and rocks, calling out to her.

"Olivia, where are you? Can you hear me? We all want you back with us. We love you and miss you a lot, and poor Mabel is heartbroken without you. Olivia, Olivia!" his voice boomed into the depths. But when he got no response, he decided to swim back to the others. He was anxious that the group did not delay in reaching fresher waters; otherwise some of the weaker members would simply die. He dreaded what he was going to say to Mabel.

Clearly Mabel was becoming weaker and more distraught with time. She was still and silent, hardly breathing, and in a deep sleep, dreaming of diamond sea slugs and glass clams.

"Mabel, wake up! Please don't give up now. Just have courage a little longer," sighed Henrietta, who swam over and tugged on the drowsy crab's pincer to wake her up.

"Leave me alone, all of you. I don't want to continue on this tiresome journey. I've simply had enough. I should have stayed in my lovely home, my treasure chest with all my precious things. Why did I listen to you?" the crab said, scowling and making a face, as she stretched her claws.

Henrietta was getting frantic and said, "Stop it at once. You are being utterly selfish and only thinking of yourself."

Mabel fixed her beady eyes on Henrietta and started sobbing.

Mike Mullet soon returned and put a comforting fin around Mabel.

"I'm so sorry, Mabel, but I had to abandon my search for Olivia. She was nowhere to be found. I swam and swam, covering fathoms of ocean in my quest for her, but my search was in vain. But you know Olivia is a clever lobster and too wise to be caught. She will look out for herself."

"Stop it at once. I don't want to hear any more. I want to lie down and go for a long sleep and never wake up. I can't bear to think of my life without Olivia," Mabel choked, in between big blobs of crab tears.

When Mike Mullet left Mabel he knew that he could not dwell on Olivia's disappearance any longer.

"Now come along, everybody. We must make headway," Mike Mullet said, trying to assemble the group together.

Henrietta sounded a note of warning to the group. "We'll never reach our destination if any of you are going to linger. Any member of this team who wanders off on their own does so at their peril. You must keep with the group – there is strength in numbers. We can all look out for each other. Travelling like this won't be forever; soon we'll arrive in the clear blue waters over there," she said, with a flick of her tail in the direction of the sunlight.

She looked at the forlorn little group around her.

"I know it's not easy, but we must try and reach fresh

waters within the next day while we still have the strength. Once there, we can all relax and eat what we like and find homes, so let's get going. I'll lead, and Mike Mullet will stay at the back and alert me if anyone is tired or weak. Mabel, please stay close to the group."

They swam on and on through the thick sandy bottom as the waters swirled around them. The tide heaved with the swell of the ocean, and creatures everywhere scurried here and there frantically on the move, bustling and rushing madly about, trying desperately to get away to fresher waters. The little group was spellbound, looking at all sorts of glowing luminous creatures darting around the waters. At one stage Henrietta was bashed up against some fierce rocks with the tidal swell and thrown wildly in the churning sea.

"Oh, I should have stayed at the wreck, where it was calm," sighed Mabel, hiding under a jutting rock to protect herself from the raging sea. She hoped to hide for a short while, but a sly sardine was watching her and alerted Mike Mullet immediately.

"Come on, Mabel, try to be brave. You will just die here on your own without us to look after you," Mike Mullet said, coaxing the difficult crab out of her little hole and persuading her to continue.

They passed some hungry seals and other dangerous predators lurking around the muddy waters on their quest for food. A large slimy conger eel enveloped Mike Mullet in his thick sinewy coils. As he tried to arch his body around the poor frightened fish and squeeze the life out of him,

Mike darted and squirmed and thrashed wildly about.

"Get away from me, you horrible ugly coiled thing!" Mike Mullet shouted, while giving the enormous eel a sharp stab of his teeth. Mike swam away, his tail thrashing, escaping the grasping coils of the horrid monster.

"My goodness, what a lucky escape. I nearly choked to death clasped by that dreadful conger," puffed Mike to Henrietta, who was clearly upset at the fate which had befallen the gentle mullet fish.

"Oh, what a horrible experience! You were so brave to give that monster a nip. He won't dare trifle with our little group again," Henrietta said, touching Mike Mullet with a gentle silver fin and brushing her mouth to his.

Then they had some luck. They met a friendly loggerhead sea turtle peddling along the waters, humming to himself.

"Hello, hello, and where are you heading, my friends?" the turtle asked in a slow soft voice. He waved a flipper at Mabel, who blushed, as nobody ever seemed to notice a crab. Crabs were not beautiful and elegant like some of the dainty silver fish.

"Oh, hello, Mr Turtle. We are all so weak and haven't eaten for days," exclaimed Mabel, waving a claw limply at him. Then Henrietta had an idea.

"Why, Mr Turtle, it's lovely to meet you. We are hoping to go to fresh waters to start a new life there. You see, we all had to leave our lovely home, an old wreck, back over there, due to an oil spillage," she said with a flick of her fin.

"Oh, I know, it's dreadful. I've just come from a place

where all the sea life has been almost wiped out," he said, drooping his large head and pointing with his great flipper in the water.

"Would you be so kind as to help one of our team? Mabel here is very weak, and she may not make it," Henrietta said, moving over to Mabel and placing a fin on her back. The kind turtle took pity on the little group.

"Of course I will. Here, climb aboard," he motioned to Mabel with a flip of his front leg.

Without thinking twice about the invitation to hop on board, Mabel heaved her ample shell onto his great hard back.

"Oh, such bliss!" sighed Mabel as she stretched herself out. The turtle swam so effortlessly through the waters that Mabel felt safe as she laid her tired and weary limbs on his huge shell. From there, she could see everything.

"Oh, this is wonderful! I can just wave to all and rest my poor weary limbs," she sighed, and stretched herself out as if she were on a vast cruise ship.

The turtle paddled along, his huge flippers like oars parting the waters. Mabel soon fell asleep on his back and was having the most wonderful crab-like dreams. After some time, the turtle stopped swimming.

"Now this is where we part company, because I am heading to warmer climes. I do wish you all the very best and hope that I was of some assistance."

Mabel suddenly awoke out of her deep sleep and stretched her weary limbs. She could have stayed on his hard back forever, but she knew that all good things come to an end.

"Thank you so much, Mr Turtle. I've got my strength back and shall now be able to keep up with the others." She heaved herself gently off and gave him a friendly pinch on his leg with her claw.

On and on the group swam until they noticed that the water was starting to flow more easily and was warmer and clearer – gone was the awful, murky, grey colour. There was plant life too.

"Oh great! Food, food and more food," exclaimed Mabel as she opened her greedy little eyes and cleaned her claws with some floating seaweed.

They then met two friendly dolphins, playing in the fresh waters. "Hello, little group," one of the dolphins clicked, as she did a backflip. This dolphin liked to show off in front of others.

"Oh, hello, we are heading out to the west to escape the oil spill. We are looking to make our new home in clear waters," said Henrietta.

"Well, you couldn't have come to a better place. I am Dora, and this is my sister Della, and we know every part of the seas around here," the dolphin clicked and did a loop. She was very much at home here. Dora noticed that Mabel could barely keep up with the group and glided over to her.

"Hop up on my back, darling, and I'll lead the way and take you to a place which is simply marvellous: full of food, safe and with as many rocks and wreck parts as you like," said Dora taking the crab by a claw. They all cheered with glee.

The little group ambled along peacefully in the calm waters, with Mabel perched on Dora's back. Dora was very playful and did all sorts of somersaults and twirls with her agile body. Poor Mabel found it hard at times to stay on the dolphin's shiny rough back.

"Dora, stop it please. I'm going to be sick, and I can barely cling on!" the poor crab shouted as she hung on for dear life with her weak pincers.

But all was to change. Suddenly they heard a loud whirring sound, and the sea seemed to heave and swirl with powerful motion. What was happening?

Then they saw it. A giant net was rolling towards them and scooping up all passing life in its way. The whole of the seabed seemed to shake with the violent movement of this great net. Dora screamed at them, "Quick, take cover! We shall all be scooped up in this huge fisherman's net."

Mabel slunk off Dora's back and fell to the bottom of the ocean, and the others in the group spread out. Henrietta let out a shriek and cried but it was too late. She found herself scooped up in the enormous net with thousands of other struggling and wriggling fish.

"Dora, Mike, please, please help me. I can't breathe!" Henrietta screamed. She tried to get to the edge of the great big ball of net to see more clearly, but she was trapped inside a giant mass of moving, swirling, silver, wriggling fish. Finally she managed to squeeze to the edge of the great hulk of net, but its holes were too narrow for her to escape. She desperately tried to wriggle out, but she had to compete with a lot of other struggling fish trying to escape as well. She felt that she was doomed to be caught up with the rest of the fish.

Peering out through a tiny hole in the net, Henrietta called out again across the great void of ocean, "Please, please, save me. Mabel, Mike Mullet, Dora, Della, where are you? I need help. It's Henrietta!"

Dora stopped suddenly. "What was that? Somebody just called my name. Listen!" Dora clicked as she turned to Della. The dolphins knew that they must act at once.

"Quick, let's go fast!" Della said frantically. They darted up to the great heaving ball of fish that was slowly being winched up to a waiting ship. They could just about see Henrietta at the edge of the net.

"Henrietta, we're coming, just hold on," Dora said. She clung to a piece of net and pulled with all her might, while Della grabbed another piece. But neither of the dolphins could break the net, as it was too strong and the weight of the giant ball of fish was too great on their jaws.

"Don't worry, Henrietta, we'll free you. I'm going to get some help," Dora said frantically and looked around. But the ball was being lifted up and soon would be out of Dora's sight. She had no time to delay. She had to act swiftly to save Henrietta. Suddenly she spied some friendly sharks darting in her direction.

"Please, please help us! Our little friend Henrietta is caught up in that great big ball of fish," Dora pleaded to one of the patrolling sharks. Then she recognised her friend, Shay. They used to swim in these same waters when they were little.

"Shay. Do you remember me, Dora?"

"Dora, of course I do!" Shay said weaving and darting.

"Hurry, we need to rescue her!" Dora gasped.

"Come on comrades!" Shay shrieked at the other sharks that were trailing him. The sharks suddenly swerved direction and darted up to the moving net, like great big shooting arrows. They tugged fiercely with their teeth in their upper jaws at the giant ball of fish. They pulled and grasped the net, but it kept rising and rising. Dora and Della looked on frantically as Henrietta's little voice faded in the distance until they could barely hear her weak calls for help, "Help, help me, please, help me…" and then they could hear her no more.

Shay and his pals tugged and ripped with their fierce teeth and all their might to free the fish imprisoned inside the great net. Suddenly it gave way and ripped asunder.

A great big mass of fish tumbled out of the bottom of the ball, and among them was dear Henrietta. She gasped and took a deep breath (as she had nearly suffocated in the net) then swam over to the two dolphins and gave each of them a kiss.

"Oh, Dora and Della, I can't thank you enough. I hated being in there, with all those squirming fish. It was horrible," the poor little herring spluttered, as she was still breathless after her frightening ordeal.

"There, there, take it easy, little one," Della said, blowing a gentle bubble in her direction.

Just as Shay and his friends were about to set off to patrol the great waters, Dora called after them, "Thanks, Shay, and your pals for helping us. Henrietta is safe and sound, and that's what's important."

Henrietta felt herself glowing all over. It was not often that a herring had the honour of thanking a great big shark such as Shay.

"Thank you so much Shay. I will always be grateful to you and to your pals for saving my life and countless others," she said shyly.

With that, Shay waved his fin and was gone.

In the distance lay a magnificent thirty metre mass of solid rock that had become separated from the mainland by a violent storm many hundreds of years ago. Beyond that lay some jagged rocks jutting up out in the ocean. The creatures could soon feel the tug and swell of the great waves as they lashed against the hulk of massive rock. Here, the sun's rays shone, plankton swirled in the sea currents, and seaweed drifted and swayed in the waters. Henrietta opened her mouth wide in this sea of plenty to take in all of the nutrients which came her way and to gorge on passing plankton.

"I see that there are lots of interesting ledges and crevices here. I am going to have a fantastic time exploring the area," exclaimed Mike Mullet, as he darted off poking and nosing his way into all the crevices.

They all thanked Dora and Della, who waved their fins at the group as they parted. "Goodbye, little ones. It was a pleasure accompanying you on your journey. Don't worry, we'll see you again. We're always around here," the dolphins clicked and squeaked, as they did some somer-saults and then disappeared.

The little creatures soon settled down to life in this

pleasant part of the sea. It was blissful being out there, sheltering in the shallow reefs, rocks and gullies. The sun shone down on the clear blue waters, and the waves gushed and lashed against the monstrous cliffs, but the creatures were as happy as could be, and none had any regrets about moving. However, they all missed Olivia and wondered what had happened to the carefree little lobster.

Olivia's Adventures

Mabel was very lonely and sad after losing her best friend Olivia. Nothing seemed to cheer her up. Henrietta tried tempting her with the most savoury delicacies that the ocean offered, but she just clammed shut her jaws and refused to eat.

"I am not hungry. I am much too sad for food. I can't bear to think of life without my dear friend Olivia," the distraught crab said and wept great tears.

"I'm so worried about Mabel. She is sad and tired all the time and just sits there, staring into the water. She won't eat and is no fun at all. It's just not like her," Henrietta said to her friend, Mike Mullet.

"I think that we need to try and find Olivia. I'll speak with Genevieve, my jellyfish friend, and hopefully she and her little band can try and find out something. They seem to know what's going on everywhere. Olivia can't have disappeared. Dora and Della have also promised me that they will keep an eye out for her, and they cover vast areas of the sea," Mike Mullet said with a movement of his head.

One day, not long after they had settled in, Genevieve

and her jelly friends, who were always trying to find out who had moved in and who was leaving, were exploring some bits of seaweed that looked interesting, when she spied a shape moving slowly along the shallow end of a reef. She drifted down to the ocean bed to find out more. Why, it was a young lobster that was clearly having difficulty with its right claw. On closer inspection, Genevieve could see that the claw was badly injured.

"Hello, Lobster, can I help you? You seem to be struggling," she said.

The lobster hardly moved. In fact Genevieve thought it might be dead. Then the lobster's antennae flicked slightly.

"Oh, that's better, at least there is some life, and where there is life, there is hope," whispered Genevieve, who always looked on the bright side of things.

Without a claw, Genevieve knew that this lobster's life hung on a fine thread. She had to get help immediately. "I've got to find Mabel. She's so clever and wise, she'll know what to do," and so the elegant jellyfish floated off, amid a sea of bubbles, in search of Mabel.

Genevieve found the crab munching on some juicy slugs and sea lettuce that she kept hidden for the odd snack. Mabel looked up and saw Genevieve swirling around her. Mabel peered at the jellyfish, her great big tentacles bobbling out from her underbelly in pink, blue, violet and orange.

"You know, Genevieve, I don't really like you and your kind, but I must admit, you are a fabulous-looking creature, with all your insides floating and hanging around you in the loveliest of colours, just like a rainbow. My, my, you make a great sight."

"Why, thank you, Mabel," said Genevieve, slightly irritated. "Err, Mabel, I wonder if you would come with me."

"Oh dear, why do you all have to disturb me just as I am tucking into a nice little snack?" Mabel said grumpily.

"I may have seen Olivia, at least it followed her description, and she may be wounded," Genevieve said. "What did you say? Olivia? Where, where? We must find her!" Mabel nearly choked on her sea lettuce.

"It's over a bit to the east where I saw the lobster; I can take you there with my friends, but it looked in a bad way."

"I'm quite ready, and we should not lose a minute more," said Mabel rising up to her full crab height. Mabel followed this swirling mass of jellyfish as they floated and bobbed in the clear waters around her. The jellyfish pirouetted down to the depths of the ocean like delicate ballerinas and approached the lobster one by one, so as not to frighten it. Mabel waddled over and poked the lobster with a claw.

The crab let out a croak of delight. "Why, it is Olivia! Oh, Olivia, my best buddy, am I glad to see you!" Mabel chirped as she peered at her poor friend.

"Are you sure it's Olivia? It's been a while since you've seen each other," Genevieve said, amid a swirl of bubbles.

"Don't be silly – of course it's Olivia. She's just had a bad time and is not well. You leave me alone with her, and she'll come around. We can then look at the claw and see what we can do. I have all kinds of ways to deal with injured claws…goodness knows, haven't I been in enough scrapes myself over the years to know what to do!" Mabel muttered.

Genevieve seemed to trust Mabel. She had heard it said among the sea creatures that she was a very wise old crab. So she swirled and swam away delighted that she had done her good deed for the day.

After some time of coaxing and whispering to Olivia, the lobster moved her antennae and said feebly, "Mabel, I am so glad to see you. Finding you again is what kept me going, despite my poor wretched claw. I enquired about our little group everywhere I went, and all the creatures were so helpful, guiding me here to where you have all settled," Olivia said.

"There, there, don't fret. There's plenty of time to tell us what happened to you, but now you must concentrate on getting this poor claw fixed, as without it, you'll never be able to scuttle around again, search for food or poke around in holes…and we couldn't have that, now, could we? You follow me to my nest, and I'll bandage up your claw," Mabel said.

Olivia relaxed and followed her dear friend Mabel to her comfortable nest under a large ledge on a bed of seaweed. Olivia stretched out and let all her weary limbs relax.

"Are you comfortable now, Olivia?" Mabel asked as she set about splinting the claw with some pieces of wood and then strapping it with seaweed.

"Oh yes. I feel so calm and relaxed, thank you Mabel," Olivia said. Mabel fed the lobster some nice juicy snacks of molluscs and clams.

"You lobsters are like us crabs. You'd eat just about anything that was given to you, as most of you are greedy just like us," Mabel said, feeding Olivia all kinds of treats.

When Olivia was feeling better and resting on a nice soft bed of sand, having gorged herself on ocean worms and slugs, she began to relax. In her painful whine, sounding just like an out-of-tune violin, she whispered to Mabel.

"I've got to tell you what happened to me when I left the little group. Oh, I don't know where to start..." she sighed, munching on another mollusc which Mabel had fed to her.

"Take it easy, and when you're ready, tell me what happened. I promise that anything you tell me will be kept a secret." But Olivia and all the other creatures knew that Mabel could never keep a secret; she was known to be one of the biggest gossips around.

"As you know, we lobsters are very curious. So I had to stop and inspect every hole and inlet that came my way. I just wandered off wherever my curiosity took me. Down and down I went until I was in the darkest and coldest waters of the deep. I was delighted as I made my way up a large beam of rotting wood, which looked like a ship's mast from an upturned shipwreck.

"I simply adore scuttling inside old wrecks, laden with goodies. It was a great big hulk of a ship lying on its side. So I clambered onto it and, with my antennae, probed the ship's compasses, sundials and instruments with compli-cated clocks."

"Oh, I love being surrounded by interesting things," Mabel sighed, reflecting on her long-lost treasure chest.

"Well, there was furniture, velvet sofas and winged armchairs inside the ship. Oh, and there was a great big bed and an enormous bath made of jade stone. I thought I was the luckiest lobster in the whole ocean to be sur-rounded by such treasures. Finally, exhausted, I waddled inside a huge wooden crate and fell asleep among casks of wines and brandy."

"Wow, this sounds like an amazing adventure," Mabel said, tucking into a periwinkle and wishing that she had accompanied Olivia.

"The next day I panicked and realised that I had to follow the sinking sun in the west and go out into the wide ocean if I was ever to meet up with you again. So I travelled slowly. I don't know how – I just kept following the sun's path as it moved in the sky during the day. I didn't have much time to eat as I was anxious to make headway, which is unusual for a lobster as we're such greedy creatures. But then I began to feel weak and tired, and I found that my poor claws could not really move with the same strength."

"One day, feeling quite dazed, due to lack of food, I ventured into a dreaded lobster pot!"

"Oh no, you didn't!" screamed Mabel, so loudly that some sea ferns nearby wobbled with alarm.

"Once in, I knew that I was doomed. How could I have been so stupid? My mother had always warned me to beware of food which came too easily. Inside this narrow cramped pot were crabs and an enormous crayfish who practically took up the entire pot. The crabs were going mad, quarrelling and fighting and blaming each other. I thought I would go insane listening to the lot of them.

"All we could do was to await the arrival of our captors. We remained silent in the pot as it swayed and churned with the seas. That dreadful crayfish was full of doom, talking about having our claws tied and being boiled alive. I simply couldn't listen to him, so I moved to the far corner of the pot, and some of the smaller crabs told him to shut up. After many hours, just before dawn, we heard the distant put-put of an outboard engine."

"What a nightmare, Olivia," Mabel said, gulping in some water.

"The pot was hauled in, and I gasped with terror as a clumsy greasy hand pulled me out of the pot. I flapped and fought with all my might and curled and uncurled my fan-like tail," Olivia said, stroking her elegant fan tail with a claw.

"The boat tilted in the waves and then heaved in the swell of the rough sea. The man was getting ready to tie my claws and end my freedom forever. I had heard it from other lobsters that I would be bound, I would be weighed and people would then eat my lovely delicate flesh. I had to act swiftly."

"Oh, the suspense is killing me!" shrieked Mabel, as she lifted out another periwinkle from its tiny shell with her large pincer.

"Mabel, I don't know where the strength came from, but I gave the man a nasty nip with my right claw and flapped my tail, and he let out a yell and dropped me. The pain was unbelievable as I hit the hard oily floor of the boat. I slid over to the far side of the boat. The sea was rough, and the boat rocked in the swell. As the man reached over to grab me, he somehow lost his balance and fell and hit his head against a jutting beam. He cried out and then fell on to the floor. The boat dipped and rose in the waves and, in doing so, water flowed into my side of the boat. I think one of the crabs got away, but the big crayfish had his claws tied. I knew I had to get away before the fisherman woke up. So I scuttled up to the edge of the boat at the front and, as the prow dipped again in the water, I paddled for my life in the shallow waters. With one big heave of my body, I was out in the wild seas, bobbing around. 'Oh, freedom at last!' I called to some squawking seagulls that were hovering overhead.

"'Well done, little lobster! Swim away as fast as you can,' they shrieked down at me and then fluttered over the boat.

"What an adventure! You were so lucky, Olivia, to escape, but don't dwell on the awful past. You must get better and get that claw fixed." They clasped each other with their large awkward claws, just like old friends.

The creatures were all thrilled when Mabel and Olivia finally made their way back to the little group.

When Olivia had fully recovered after a few weeks, Henrietta said, her eyes perky with excitement, "Listen, I've got a super idea. Why don't we invite all our new pals and get to know more creatures from the deep? After all, we need to make friends and find out more about our neighbours."

"That's a great idea," Mabel hissed, who always got excited at the mention of a party and food. Mabel was only happy when her ample belly was full of nice savoury titbits.

"That's wonderful. Olivia's return calls for a real celebration," piped up Mike Mullet, blowing bubbles and flicking his tail and fins.

So Henrietta, Mike Mullet, Mabel and Olivia planned a welcoming party. They got help with preparing for the event. Mabel was in charge of the food. Genevieve and her jellyfish and some helpful mackerel sent around the invitations. "Let's hope that lots of friends and neighbours can make it," said Henrietta looking at the seabed and wondering who would turn up to their little party.

"We can get the invites delivered by some passing turtles, flat fish or drifting jellyfish," Mike Mullet said.

So the day of the party came and there was great excitement and preparation as a great feast was laid out on a huge rock, with all kinds of tempting goodies.

"The messengers must be reliable. We can't have fish falling asleep or leaving to go off with another shoal," piped up Mike Mullet.

"Hear, hear! I want this party to be a good one and to make sure that everybody knows about it. So let's all put our best efforts into making it a success," Henrietta said. Enthusiastic young sardines darted around great coral banks or under clumps of giant weeds to distribute the invitations, which were made out on long bits of seaweed in special fish language. The seaweed was rolled up and also delivered on the backs of turtles, and flat fish distributed them to all those who lived on the seabed. Nothing was left to chance.

"I am determined, for Mabel and Olivia's sake, that the party shall be success," Henrietta confided to Mike Mullet. He nodded, as he knew how disappointed the little group would be if the party was a flop.

On the day of the party, local shrimps took charge of draping different coloured algae and seaweed over a massive rock by a reef, and ferns swayed in the sea, popping out invitations to any passing creatures.

Mabel took charge of the menu and she was helped by some cheery eels and hardworking young sprats. "Now, my dears, please pay attention and listen carefully to what I am going to tell you. I am determined that this party is going to be brilliant, the best party ever held underwater. You fill some cockle-shell bowls with rich plankton, and then pile them high with green, brown and red seagrass. Let me show you," Mabel said, as she filled up the bowls with various goodies.

The small fish stared in amazement as Mabel deftly demonstrated exactly how she wanted the bowls to be presented. After a while, she spied a young lazy sprat that had not been paying sufficient attention to detail. She tottered up on her claws and filled her gills, puffed herself up and said, "Not that way, you clumsy young fish. Appearance is so important. You just can't serve bowls of food like that. This is a party, for heaven's sake. Oh, I don't know. Nobody teaches anybody anything anymore."

However, most of the helpers were very fond of Mabel and didn't mind her getting angry with them. She was only doing what was best. Finally all of the sand buns were stuffed with various delicacies. Some sporty sea snakes served fern and algae juices in periwinkle shells and cockle urns.

At last it was time for the celebrations. Olivia arrived first on the fin of Mike Mullet, who was clearly enchanted with the delightful young lobster.

"Why, you look stunning, Olivia!" he murmured, complimenting her on her outfit. Olivia wore a dress made

of red algae. This elegant gown was draped over her front, creating quite a dash, and on her front pincers she wore stylish sea-foam gloves with water pearls and tiny bits of coloured seaweed hung from her antennae. Mike Mullet went and got her a drink, and they glided around the party, greeting all the other creatures. They were followed by a few young silver fish, who liked to go to all social events.

Mabel arrived wearing some curly sea ferns clasped onto her back. She was entranced as she cast her beady eyes over the splendid repast which lay before her.

"My, my, what a great banquet. I won't have to eat for at least a week," she chuckled, helping herself when nobody was looking to a sand bun filled with slugs.

"Yum, yum, all smells delicious. I have been starving myself all day so that I can eat as much as I like," she smirked as she surveyed the delicious spread with her beady little eyes. She then tucked into a clam sandwich. It was so delicious that she grabbed another and then another.

But Henrietta was the most beautiful of all. She was draped with a magnificent gown of silver sea-threads woven from the finest weed, which matched her silver skin, and shone like mirrors in the shallow waters. She sipped some

plankton from a coral urn and met many creatures of the sea that night.

Genevieve and her jellyfish trio played jazzy music on their special fern guitars, and the rich sounds spread through the ocean's depths. Olga the octopus performed a belly dance, and a big ugly conger eel gaped at all the party activities from his secret cave.

At one stage, the eel was eyeing up Olga to take a bite at her, but she sprayed him with some ink, and he got such a fright that he returned to his cave. Two seahorses sang

a sad lullaby, and some young, energetic cod made booming sounds with funny-looking instruments made of shells and driftwood. The creatures danced and partied until the laughing moon disappeared at the first light of dawn.

As the sun came up and its rays spread down into the sea and onto the tired sea creatures, Henrietta swam over to Mabel and Olivia who were tucked comfortably among the rocks in the shallow water.

"So, ladies, how are you?" the little silver fish asked.

"Well, we've had a wonderful time and have met so many new friends – what a great party! But we must take a rest now," Olivia said, stretching one of her large claws and nearly causing poor Henrietta to flip. Olivia tottered off and tucked herself away in her snug-like grotto among the rocks.

"I have never enjoyed myself so much, Henrietta, and I am so, so happy that we moved here, and I am among friends again in a beautiful part of the ocean. Thank you for being such an inspiration and for guiding us here. We are all ever so grateful," Mabel said, as she gave the little herring a great big hug.

"Why, thank you, Mabel. It's so nice to hear that!" Henrietta said, dabbing a tear from her eye.

"I must go to sleep now, as it has been a long night," Mabel said as she crawled under a heap of sand and fell asleep, dreaming of the wonderful delicacies she had just devoured.

The remainder of the guests drifted back to their homes in the silent waters. Henrietta thought of her friends in the wreck whom she had left behind when the oil slick came, and she wished that some of them could have been with them to share in the festivities that night. But she had no regrets about leaving the thick treacle sea around the wreck. She was so glad that she had settled down in this lovely part of the ocean with her friends.

Sea creatures and fishes swam to and fro in these calm and peaceful waters, but Henrietta, Mabel, Olivia and Mike Mullet lived out the remainder of their lives happily among the jagged rocks and white foam in that lovely little corner of the sea.

The Golden Plumes

Michael lived far away up in the mountains with his parents. He was twelve years old and an only child. Each day he had to travel across rugged countryside to go to school. It took him nearly two hours each way, but he enjoyed the journey as he could admire the breath-taking views from the craggy mountainside and listen to the wildlife.

He loved to watch the soaring eagles as they hovered in the air, and then swooped on their prey.

His father and grandfather always protected these great birds; leaving out the spoils for the birds from their hunting expeditions in times of plenty. They left the tall trees and land undisturbed for the eagles' continued existence.

Michael loved the eagles more than any other wild creature or bird. When young boys from the village climbed the tall trees or cliffs to steal the birds' eggs from their nests, he would recover the eggs and replace them to their rightful place, even if it meant the odd fight and punch up with these boys. His father had made a harness for him, so that he could climb the tallest trees. He would strap the harness around his waist and throw up a rope onto a sturdy branch and then lever himself up. Neither had he any fear of scaling the sheerest of cliffs. He liked to peep into these great big eagle nests and watch the maturing and growth of the young chicks, as they gobbled down whole mice and voles and great chunks of raw meat brought to them by their parents. His father had told him that these birds were rare and sacred and would soon be no more, if they were hunted to extinction.

One day on Michael's way to school, some boys from a nearby village set upon him. They were jealous of him, as he was clever at school and good at sport. As they punched and kicked him, a great eagle soared in the air. With the

bird's All-Seeing Eye, it swooped down and flapped its wings and shrieked, digging its huge talons into one of the boys and frightened them away.

Michael was badly injured from the punches and kicks and could hardly move. He lay on the side of the mountain, bruised and sore from his injuries. As he lay there, an eagle

approached him, hovered for a while, and then turned and disappeared over the tall pines. After some time, the great bird returned carrying a small tin of fresh stream water in its beak.

Soon the eagle was feeding the injured boy some wild berries. At night the eagle circled over the young boy to keep watch on him and ensure that no danger befell him.

During the day, the eagle flapped its enormous wings to keep him cool from the harsh rays of the sun.

On the third day, as the sun rose, Michael stretched himself and had regained his strength and was well enough to return home. As he got up, he caught sight of six golden

plumes on the ground beside him. Each plume was about as long as a dagger with a white central spine and flanked on each side with fine golden feathers tapering to white.

"Why they are eagles' feathers!" he exclaimed. They seemed to shine and change colour as the young boy tilted them in the in the sunlight.

"Oh what beauties! I have never seen anything so magnificent. But what am I to do with them? What do they signify? Why were they left here?" he wondered.

He wrapped the plumes in some long leaves growing nearby and tucked them under his arm and made his way slowly back home with the help of a large stick he had found. He had difficulty climbing the hills, but the eagles flew constantly overhead and this reassured him.

His parents were delighted when he returned, as they had been worried that they would never see him again, as they knew that he had enemies out there who wanted to do him harm. He ran and hugged them and told them what had happened.

"Oh, Michael, we are thrilled to see you. We sent out a search party for you. We had given up all hope, and now you are here," his mother sobbed as she held him close to her. His father took a whiff of his pipe, put down his book and came over and clasped his boy to him.

"We must never let you go that route on your own again. I shall accompany you to school from now on and we shall take Lara with us. We shall catch those boys and punish them for nearly leaving you half dead." Lara was their dog, a big hairy scraggy sheep-dog who would defend and protect them on their journey.

"But Papa, an eagle saved me. He flew down and shrieked and dug his claws into one of those boys. I was so frightened, but then they ran off. Soon the great bird came back with some water and berries. I would have died on the side of the mountain only for the eagle," Michael said with tears in his eyes, as he looked up at the sky and wondered if he might see one of these magnificent creatures. "Ah, the great golden eagles of the mountainside. It is a pity that the farmers hunt them, to protect their livestock," the father said, looking at his son.

The father continued. "It is true what they say though, that these birds are wise beyond their species and years. They are truly the majestic giants of the sky, overseeing all living things."

"Oh Papa, I have something to show you, come with me," the boy said eagerly grabbing his father's hand and taking him to his room. There he unfurled the long grasses inside of which were the six golden plumes.

The father picked up one golden plume with its white tip and examined it intensely. "I wonder if we could write with it," he murmured.

"Let's see," said Michael taking the golden plume from his father's hand. He placed the quill in his right hand and scratched on a piece of paper. As he wrote some letters, beautiful shiny golden ink flowed from its tip. The boy's hand couldn't stop writing. He had this desire to continue, as if he couldn't stop. His hand seemed to be propelled to write by some unknown strange force. The letters in golden ink sparkled on the paper and appeared to change shade; sometimes becoming deep rich gold with flashes of ruby, reminding him of the sunset. Other times, the ink wrote with a pale gold like straw, but Michael's favourite was the ink as colourful as the wild honey his father made. Then he drew swirls and decorations with curls and loops and strange shapes, just like he had seen on the ancient manuscripts in the museum. Finally exhausted, he laid down the plume and rested his hand.

The father scratched his head and said, "These are indeed special plumes. We must arrange for an expert to look at them. We must guard the plumes and keep them safely." His father turned and looked around as if wondering where to hide them.

After much debate, they decided to bury the plumes under the kitchen floor where they would be secure. There the temperature was neither too hot nor too cold and no thief would ever suspect their presence under the floor in the kitchen. So they removed a few tiles and wrapped the six plumes in fine gauze and then carefully lay them down on the cold ground before replacing the tiles.

Each evening after school, Michael unearthed the golden plumes and drew on slate, paper or on anything he could find. The plumes continued to write with the most exquisite letters and different shades of silky golden ink. He wrote poems and stories about what he did that day or the animals he had encountered, but mostly he wrote from his creative imagination. Vivid thoughts and ideas sprang from him onto the page and he started to produce short stories full of life and vibrancy. These were stories of strange ethereal creatures from another world, which dwelt and lived deep inside caves under the sea. Other stories were of powerful gods whose majesty commanded and ruled the skies. The young boy was so happy writing with his new-found plumes. He tried out a different one every day and they all poured out the same wonderful flowing golden ink.

Michael mounted the golden script and shapes onto canvas and his father framed these drawings. They brought his works of art to various booksellers in the local market. His short stories were compiled into a small booklet, bound with a leather cover encrusted with golden images created by the plumes.

Soon the magic of the plumes became known in the area and the surrounds, as people spied the beautiful golden writing and wondered about the creative artist who had produced such wonderful works of art.

One day, a professor from the local university, who had heard of the famous plumes, visited their house to examine these wondrous objects. He was an authority on ancient manuscripts and ancient languages.

He held a plume aloft in the sun, turned it, felt its feathers, put it up to his nose and smelt it and then wrote some words of an ancient script on writing paper with it.

"Ah, this is truly wonderful. But how did you come to be in possession of such a beautiful natural gift?" the Professor asked.

His father thought for a moment and said, "One day my son Michael was attacked by some local youths and they injured him quite badly and left him dead. But he was helped by one of the golden eagles of which we have some pairs nesting up in the high mountains.

Michael looks after their nests and ensures that if their eggs are stolen that they are returned and he does his utmost to protect them. My brother and I leave out meat from our hunting expeditions, so we feel that in some strange way, Michael has been rewarded for his care to these great giants of the sky."

The Professor thought for a moment. "Indeed, that is a very likely explanation for the origin of these plumes, but how can they produce this wonderful golden ink? That is the question, to which I cannot find any answer.

It is indeed extraordinary and something which we may never find out. I shall discuss these plumes with some of my eminent colleagues." The Professor left, still baffled by the wonders of the plumes.

But one evening, as the family took to the mountainside to check on their sheep with Lara, thieves crept into the house and prised open the tiles and quietly made off with the six golden plumes. Somehow, they had heard about them and their magic properties. The thieves had carefully replaced the tiles, giving the impression that nothing unusual had taken place in the kitchen.

"We can sell them and make money and we will never be poor again," the thieves murmured as they made off with the prize plumes, hurrying down the mountainside.

When Michael returned and lifted up the tiles, he was horrified that nothing was there but the gauze wrapping.

"Oh my beautiful plumes, where you are?" He cried and cried, and his parents could do nothing to console him.

"We'll make enquiries, but there is little point in offering a reward for something as precious as these plumes. They are priceless," his dad said resignedly.

When the thieves tried to write with the plumes, nothing came out of the quills. They were as dry as the sand in the desert.

As the weeks went by, the thieves grew tired of staring at the dried up plumes. One day, in a furious rage, they pitched the plumes out of the window from their house and the feathers scattered in the wind which took them off in various directions.

One of the plumes landed on the road with the busy traffic and was flattened by fleeting cars, but still managed to survive and let the wind take it up and away, swirling in the air. Another plume sailed down the river and floated onto the feathers of a passing heron, ending up on the riverbank when the bird dived underwater. A flying crow picked up another which briefly formed part of her nest. The rest of the plumes slowly drifted from high office towers to suburban gardens, to railway lines or to the busy streets where they were trampled upon; their beauty hardly noticed by the passing crowds. However, after several months of flying and fluttering around, all of the plumes somehow made their way back, soaring up to the mountains, to the young boy's house, as if guided by some strange magical powers.

One day, as Michael was heading out for school, a golden plume fell at his feet and he picked it up.

"Oh! One of the lost plumes, am I glad to see you?" He thought that the eagles might have had something to do with their return. He rushed inside to see if it could still write with the silky golden ink and sure enough, the page was soon filled with the most beautiful lettering, as before. Within a couple of weeks, the other five plumes fluttered their way back to the house.

Michael and his parents were overjoyed that all of the plumes had flown home again.

"We shall guard these plumes well and ensure that nothing happens to them. They are too precious," his father murmured. They bought a huge big safe that nobody could open, except with a special code and to this day, Michael writes the most wonderful works in golden ink, which are shown and admired worldwide.

Tammy

Tammy, the crow, had reared her brood for the year. She could rest now, as her three young crows had learned to fly away and had left the nest. Tammy had plenty of time to watch out for danger and to help the other birds and creatures of the wood.

One bright evening, while hopping around in a field full of turnips, Tammy spied, with her beady eye, a small black and grey furry animal lying under the hedge at the edge of the field. Being the curious bird that she was, she hopped over to find out more. Why, it was a baby badger! She could tell from the black and white stripes running down each side of his sad face. As she approached, she could hear groaning. Upon looking closer at the small bundle of fur, she gasped:

"Why, poor little thing! You seem to be injured!"

She strutted around to its side and noticed that the young badger had a big gash on its left leg, which was bleeding. The badger seemed to be in a lot of pain. It lay there, breathing rapidly with its mouth open, desperately trying to take in enough air for its weak lungs.

Peering into its sad eyes, Tammy whispered, "Hello, little one. I'm Tammy. I really do want to help you."

The badger lifted his head slightly and replied feebly, "Hello, Tammy. I'm very hungry, as I haven't eaten for days, and I feel very weak."

He let his head down gently on his limp paws. Tammy came closer and listening intently, asked, "What happened to you that you are lying here like this? And how did you injure that leg? It looks very bad to me."

He coughed a little and opened his mouth feebly. "Well, some days ago a group of men came with dogs to our sett, and they killed all of my family. One of the dogs attacked me and bit my leg, but I managed to escape and hid for days until it was safe to come out."

Tammy was moved.

"Oh dear. You poor darling. How sad. That looks like a nasty gash on your leg," said the motherly crow. Being the practical bird that she was, Tammy knew how important a good healthy diet was. "Now the first thing I need to do is to get you some nice juicy worms. By eating nourishing food, you'll get your strength back, and it will help your leg to heal."

She then hopped off to the nearest turnip row in the quest for some fat wriggly earthworms. As she gathered up some tasty worms, she met her friend Annie, a pheasant, who was picking away at the ground.

"Hello, Annie," chuckled Tammy. But Annie hardly noticed Tammy, so intent was she on filling her crop.

"Yum, yum, these turnip tops are delicious. I simply

can't eat enough of them," the pheasant said as she hungrily gobbled up the turnip heads. "Well, I'm actually looking for some juicy worms," the kind crow said.

"Oh, well, there are plenty of worms around, and lots and lots of insects and grubs. Goodbye and best of luck with your search." And Annie flew off to another part of the field.

When Tammy had collected enough worms and insects, she went back to the baby badger and placed the food in front of him.

"Now, little one, eat up these delicious worms to get better. Then I'll get you more."

The badger raised himself up and sniffed at the worms. "Yum, these worms sure smell good," he said, and with one snap of his jaws he swallowed the lot. Tammy watched him in wonder.

"Thanks, Tammy," he piped up.

But Tammy was still curious about him. "What is your name?"

"I was known as Barney in my family."

"Barney the badger! What a lovely name – it really suits you. Now I must fly off and get you some more fat worms to make you better."

Tammy flew off into the field to look for more food for Barney. This routine continued for several days until the young badger started to get well and regain his strength. Each morning, Tammy flew from her perch in the tall Scotch pine tree to check on Barney. She would then fly to the field to get some fresh food for him. At night Barney hid in the bushes and covered himself well to keep safe and away from danger. Thankfully, those men with their dogs never returned.

After a week the wound on Barney's leg had almost healed. With his strength back, he was able to lick it clean. He started to walk slowly again, limping at first, and all the time the loyal crow kept by his side, alerting him to danger and bringing him his food. Tammy looked after him as if he were one of her own brood.

After some time resting and eating, Barney was well

enough to venture off and hunt for himself. The nights were warm and there was plenty of food. He needed to vary his diet and explore the land. He took it easy at first, preferring not to go too far for fear of danger. He travelled over a few fields and fed on grubs, worms and insects to regain his strength. He passed farmhouses nestling in the fields, with their lights shining, but he just moved silently on.

Sometimes he met Ferdia, the fox. Ferdia could evade guns and hounds and was able to wriggle and bury himself under the tightest of wire. He could chew through the toughest wood or fencing. Ferdia was able to travel for miles at night, raiding henhouses and duck ponds. One evening, as they sat together in the moonlight, Ferdia was resting after an evening of thieving and destruction.

"Are you never afraid of the farmers with their dogs and their shotguns?" Barney asked the fox. Ferdia licked his lips and, gazing up at the moon gliding through the clouds, he sighed. Then he replied, "We foxes live on our wits. We

62

don't have time to think of the dangers lurking out there."
The fox was so shrewd that he rarely went hungry; he was
able to ferret out food all year round with his wily ways.

With a resigned air, the fox got up, dusted himself
down and slunk off into the night. Barney thought he
looked magnificent in the moonlight with his fine glossy
coat and bushy tail.

Tammy was delighted that Barney had finally recovered
now that autumn was here. Winter came, and with it the
frost arrived, and the badger and crow remained the best
of friends. The following spring Tammy was busy making
preparations to build a new nest, and during her quest for
sticks and lining for the nest, she came across Barney. He
had grown strong and healthy with a fine shiny coat.

"What are your plans, Barney, now that spring is here?"

Barney moved closer to Tammy and whispered to her,
"Can I tell you a secret?"

Tammy, who loved being asked to keep a secret, moved
closer and chuckled gleefully, "Do tell..."

"I've met another badger, and her name is Dusty."

Tammy was thrilled with this bit of gossip. "Oh, Barney,
I'm so happy for you! That is really wonderful news. You
deserve to meet a nice badger; after all you've been through."

"Dusty is a beauty. I met her one night when wandering on my journey for food. She is young and healthy,
with a sleek and glossy coat. She is from a large badger sett
nearby."

"Oh how I love a bit of romance!" Tammy said, as she
hopped around him, giggling and chuckling.

"We plan to move just a few miles away to the bog beyond the wood. There the ground is soft and rich with food, and there is no farmhouse around for miles."

"Oh I know it quite well, where that quiet herd of champagne coloured cattle chomp and chew their cuds all day long," Tammy said flapping her wings.

Tammy was so happy that she danced around the field and then flew off into the woods to consider this latest piece of news. Barney had grown into a fine, strong, healthy badger and was clearly ready to settle down, establish his sett and start a family.

But then one day Tammy just disappeared. None of the creatures in the wood had seen her. Barney asked Ferdia Fox and Harry Hedgehog if they had seen the generous crow, but they shook their heads and went about their business. Barney had heard guns recently in the woods and feared the worst. Autumn was the start of the shooting season.

Poor Tammy had been busy hopping around and alerting all the creatures to the dangers from the guns. Then one chilly and frosty morning she got hit on her side by some gun pellets and could not move, as her wing was injured. For days she lay on the cold ground in agony, terrified to cry out, all the while getting weaker and weaker.

A few days after her accident, when she was nearing her end, two young girls, Laura and Katie, were out walking with their dad. They saw Tammy lying on the ground. Picking up the injured bird, they called to their father,

"Dad, the poor bird's wing is broken and it can't fly."

"Don't interfere with nature. Better leave it alone,

and besides it's probably covered in lice... It'll die anyway, and the sooner the better, for its own sake," their dad shouted after them.

But the little girls were not happy with this explanation, and Katie examined the wing further. Tammy was quivering with fear and pain.

"Poor little thing! You are so frightened. We won't hurt you."

"Please, please, Dad, can we take it back home with us? The poor thing will die a horrible slow death if we leave it lying here in the cold," Laura pleaded with him.

"But what about Gemma? That cat will smell it as soon as you bring it home and then go for it as soon as your back is turned," their dad said poking a stick under Tammy's wing. Now Tammy was absolutely terrified. She might as well just curl up and die. But the little girls persisted and finally persuaded their father to take Tammy home with them, wrapping her in a scarf. She was so weak that she fainted in the car. She missed the familiar sounds and smells of the wood.

Katie and Laura took Tammy to the vet in a shoebox lined with straw. The vet strapped her wing and gave them some painkillers. He taught the girls how to feed the bird with a tiny syringe. Tammy was placed into a large cage perched high up in a small room off the kitchen. The girls were kind and did not handle her too much, except to feed her and check on her broken wing. Gemma, a huge fat marmalade puss, could barely get through the cat-flap, so large was her waist. She spent her time staring up at

Tammy in the cage, while making all kinds of noises and faces. Tammy hated the sight of this wretched cat with her evil grin and twitching whiskers.

Instead of a beautiful blue dome of a sky, Tammy had only a greasy spotty ceiling from years of cooking. The children's mother banged pots and pans in the kitchen around meal times. Tammy soon started eating bread and cheese. How she longed for fresh insects and worms, and the seeds, nuts and fat balls that she would feed on from the bird tables in people's gardens.

One day when all the family had gone out, the cat slyly hid under the kitchen furniture and sneaked up on the ledge and stealthily pawed her way to Tammy's cage. Tammy hopped and screamed round the cage, setting crumbs and water flying in all directions.

"Get away, you despicable thing! You come any further and I'll peck out your mean green eyes," she screeched at the surprised cat. Gemma became alarmed with Tammy's shrieking and hissing and lost her balance. She fell, crashing onto the kitchen table, knocking down a vase of flowers and sending cups and saucers flying. The cat landed on the hard stone floor in front of the fridge and hobbled off. As she made her way out, Tammy shouted insults after her, "You vile creature! Don't you ever, ever attempt to claw your way into my cage or I'll jab and poke you with my sharp claws, so I will!"

Tammy's strength returned slowly but surely, and her wing no longer hurt. She was able to move it slightly and each day flapped her wings and did exercises. One day she

knew that she would be ready to make her final escape from this cage.

Katie and Laura took Tammy out into the garden sometimes. She was glad to get away from the greasy and steamy smells of the kitchen. One day in late summer, the children started to clean Tammy's cage.

They brought the cage out into the garden to give it

a thorough wash. Laura held Tammy gently while Katie cleaned and scrubbed the inside of the cage. She put down fresh newspapers, clean water and bird seed for Tammy. Suddenly the doorbell rang and both girls fled.

They put Tammy back in the cage and closed it before speeding off to see who was at the door. But they did not close the cage properly and, in the slight wind, the door swung open. Tammy could not believe her luck. "Could this be true?" she gasped in amazement.

She knew she had to be quick with her plan of escape before the girls or that cat arrived. She hopped to the edge of the cage, took a deep breath, and sighed with relief as she touched the soft green grass. Oh, the bliss of feeling the grass on her tired feet, instead of hard, rumpled, dirty newspapers, full of her droppings! She hopped over to the lilac tree, to seek some cover, and there she would bide her time. Her movements were slow, and she was not sure if she could fly again. Peering out from the hedge, she saw a small road and some more houses on the other side of the road. She just had to be brave and go; otherwise she would simply die in that wretched cage. She squeezed under the wire near the hedge, but did not have the strength to continue. She lay there for a while to regain her breath and then ventured a little farther, each time making headway. It was hard at first, but with each little bit, she was gaining strength and confidence to continue.

Night fell, and Tammy became cold and frightened. It was all so new to her; strange sounds and smells that she was not used to. She decided to wait until dawn before attempting to fly. She flew up onto a branch of a nearby tree amid some greenery and waited for the dawn chorus. She was scared stiff as she watched and waited. Then suddenly something pounced beside her. It was a young red squirrel with a triangle of white fur on its chest and a great bushy tail.

"Hello, crow. What are you doing here? You should be up on a tall tree watching everything for miles, not down here on this little garden bush," he said.

"I am trying to escape from a house where I have spent a long time recovering with a broken wing, but I must get my strength back and fly home," Tammy said politely to the squirrel, who had his head bent and was determined to find out more.

"Where is home?" asked the eager squirrel.

"Over in the great wood beyond," Tammy murmured, lifting her wing a little to point in the direction.

"Know it well. Tomorrow morning you head to the south by that chimney pot over there, see," he said, pointing his little paw in the general direction, "and then you fly out west. I'll stay here and keep you company for tonight and make sure you come to no harm. Can I get you some nuts or worms to eat?" he asked rubbing a gentle paw over her feathers.

"Oh, thank you so much! I could do with something," Tammy sighed as she thought of fresh natural food from the earth, instead of stale bread and hard cheese. He was proving to be a nice, caring young squirrel.

The squirrel was true to his word and looked after

Tammy all night, providing her with nuts and seeds until they heard the dawn chorus, when he darted up onto a higher branch.

"Goodbye, crow, and good luck," and he disappeared into the foliage.

"Goodbye, little squirrel, and thanks," Tammy sighed, and realised she was on her own now.

Once she heard the chirruping of the birds at dawn she spread her wings confidently and lifted her head high.

"I can do it. I can fly again. Just be patient, a little bit at a time," she kept saying to herself. She hopped from branch to branch, each time getting higher and higher, until at last she could see the sky and the tops of the houses. She knew she must not overdo things, as she feared she might tire herself out. After all, her wings and muscles were stiff, as she had not used them for a long while.

Meanwhile, in the wood, all of the creatures were very sad, as they believed that Tammy had been shot by the sportsmen. The seasons passed, but there was no sign of the popular mother crow. Barney was travelling much wider afield, as he needed to feed his large family of six.

"Poor Tammy. I hope that she is all right. She is such a wonderful creature and looks out for us all here in the wood," he said, with tears in his eyes.

"I know, darling. You wouldn't be here if it wasn't for Tammy," Dusty said, putting a paw around him and giving him a big hug.

Tammy possessed a great sense of direction. All her family were very clever and rarely got lost and could travel for miles at a time. So, letting out a big squawk, she lifted her tired wings and slowly flew through the housing estate. She rested on a chimney pot and met some starlings on a nearby satellite dish. They were twittering and mimicking two magpies that were raiding a dustbin outside a house. The cheeky magpies had pulled plastic bags and tins all over the roadside.

"Dirty thieving birds," one starling said haughtily, as they looked around at the mess created by the magpies.

But Tammy couldn't be bothered listening to them and continued on her journey. She then flew south-west, as the squirrel had told her, and came out among some green fields. Here she noticed the swallows lined up on the electricity wires, getting ready for their journey back to warmer countries after the summer.

"Hi, swallows, are you set for your long trip?"

"Just about…We need to get one or two of the young ones fully trained for the long road ahead and then we're on our way," they chirruped as they looked out to the vast horizon.

"Well, good luck and keep safe." And, spreading her wings, Tammy flew off. She knew that she had a lot of area to cover before arriving at her beloved woods.

After some leisurely flying, her wings were tired, and she simply could not continue. She knew that she had to rest. She stopped on the roof of a church. She was too frightened to think of food as she tried to focus on the journey home. There would be plenty of time to think of things to eat later on. All was quiet until she met some ravens hanging around. She strutted nervously over to an elderly one, who looked wise and caring.

"Excuse me, please. Can you tell me if I am heading in the direction of the great wood?" she asked.

The raven looked at her and then peered down at her frail legs. He suspected that she had an injured wing, as she was not standing up straight. "Oh, yes, but it's a long way from here, my dear. Are you sure you can make it? Come up here to the steeple and let me show you."

Tammy hopped up the roof after him as he made his way to the great height of the steeple, but she could not venture any further.

"Stop, please stop. I can't go any higher. My wings won't let me."

She rested on the bell tower alongside the sloping roof, and the raven hopped back down to meet her.

"Are you sure you are up to flying this distance?" he asked her kindly.

"Yes, I shall be all right, but I have to take things easy. You see, I have been in a cage for a year, in a house, after I was injured, and I am not used to flying high. I'll get there with patience and hard work, though."

"Don't worry, my dear. You can take as long as you like," the kind raven said gently, and flew up into the sky overhead.

Tammy felt safe and secure resting on the thick wall enclosing the giant bell, but knew that she would have to leave soon. So with great effort she spread her wings, filled her lungs and forced herself to fly up onto the high church steeple. From there, she could see for miles around. Steadying herself on the top of the steeple, she looked up at the raven soaring high over her in the blue sky. As he swept his wing in the air and looked down at her he cried, "Can you see over there? On the other side of the hill lies the wood. You'll have to fly over the hill and about three fields beyond that. You'll find it."

"Thank you so much. You've been very kind. I'll set off now, while the sun is shining." Tammy spread her wings and, with renewed confidence, she glided off the roof and over the fields in the direction of the wood.

She found it was easy to fly. The morning air was fresh

and a light breeze propelled her along. How happy Tammy was! She was finally going home, back to all that was dear and familiar to her, to her home in the woods.

She was grateful to the two little girls who had saved her, as without their kindness she would not be here, gliding home, but would instead have died of a broken wing on that cold wintry ground.

Soon she started to see familiar sights on her journey home: the old farmhouse, whose barns she had often raided for grain; the turnip field, where she had first met poor injured Barney. And then there it was, coming out of the low cloud: her beloved tall tree where she had built her nests over the years and raised her family.

"Oh, I'm home! Home at last!" she squawked. She glided on and on until she reached her favourite Scotch pine tree, where she perched herself and took in the old familiar sights. She rested on a branch and breathed a great sigh of relief. Then she let out a great raucous caw. She was tired and needed to get her breath back, after all it had been a long, long flight home.

Word went around among the creatures of the wood that their beloved crow had returned.

"Guess what! Tammy's back!" they all chorused and whispered.

That evening all the creatures of the wood assembled under the Scotch pine tree where Tammy made her home. Barney, Dusty and their six little baby badgers joined them too. There were pigeons, thrushes, blackbirds, starlings, hedgehogs, squirrels and a family of mice. They had all come together to welcome Tammy home and to celebrate her safe return. Barney cried as he hugged the fragile crow.

"Oh, Tammy, we thought you were gone forever. I can't tell you how happy I am to see you."

Tammy's daughters, Debby and Mitsi, prepared a great feast for her homecoming. Harriet and Henry Hare came with their latest brood, as did a young family of rabbits who had moved into the old burrow by the stream. All gathered to chat and chirp and squawk and squeak until all hours. Barney cleared his throat and welcomed Tammy home.

"Tammy, we are all delighted that you have returned back to us here. We didn't know what had happened to you, but we feared the worst. You have always looked out for the creatures in the wood, alerting us to dangers and helping us when we are in difficulty." He started to cry as he recalled how Tammy had helped him when his whole family had been killed. Dusty handed him a large dock leaf to wipe his eyes. "There, there, don't get upset. After all Tammy is back and you have a young family now and I am here," she whispered. Barney continued, "It was Tammy to whom I owe an enormous debt, and we would all like to welcome you, dear Tammy, back home."

Tammy, overcome with emotion, squawked and chirped, "I can't tell you all how much I missed you and our lovely wood. Like Barney, I had been wounded, my wing was broken, and I was rescued by two kind little girls who took me to their home and nursed me back to health. But I was in captivity in a large cage, and I know that I would have died from a broken heart if I had not escaped. So escape I did one day."

She stopped and looked around and could see that all the creatures were spellbound listening to her adventures. "I was determined one day to come back here to the wood, and I am so, so, happy to be back with you all again."

A rousing chorus of cheers went up among the creatures of the wood and the party started. There was a big salad of hazelnuts, blackberries and hawthorns, served on sycamore leaves with some light moss dressing. They drank primrose juice from acorn shells, nectar from bluebells and wild honey from foxglove petals. The squirrels collected nuts and berries, and woodland mice served frosted dew on wild rose petals, while some clever toads had prepared buttercup pasties served on giant water lilies.

The bullfrogs emerged from the nearby marsh at the edge of the wood and played jazzy tunes on reeds. They all danced on a carpet of pine needles and sang under a canopy of stars. The violets, wild garlic and cowslips laughed to their hearts' content, and the stars smiled back and joined in the fun.

"Tammy, this is a fantastic party. We have not had so much fun for a long time," a young blackbird chirped excitedly.

Marigold, the tawny owl, sat up in her nest on the old oak tree and kept a watchful eye on matters. Finally they all drifted off to their nests and lairs when the blood red sun emerged. The twinkling stars returned to their dark secret caves in the eastern sky.

Time heals, and so do wounds. But Barney and Tammy were grateful to have survived their experiences and lived out the remainder of their brave little lives in the great wood. They watched out for each other and for their families, and for the other animals, especially the young, the old and the frail.

Plum Tree Castle

Long ago in a small town, there was a wonderful castle called Plum Tree Castle. It was known far and wide for its splendid gardens in which grew the most delicious plum trees. These exquisite fruit trees were famous, not only for the fat ripe plums, but also for the sweet music which they produced. As soon as one plucked a plum from one of these trees, the whole place filled with the melody of a lyre. No hunters were permitted near the castle, so gentle fawn,

rabbits, squirrels and other wildlife enjoyed many years of peace within the walls of the castle.

A young maiden called Saffron, who was confined to a wheelchair, lived at the castle with her elderly father. She had fallen from her pony Marble when jumping a high ditch when she was only a small girl and sadly had broken her back. As a result, she could never walk again. But Saffron was brave and could wheel and spin around the place in her chair without any bother. Her mother Caroline had died many years ago from the bite of a poisonous insect in the garden. In Caroline's memory, the plum trees played the sweetest tunes each time a fruit was picked or dropped to the ground. So when the fruits were at their ripest, the garden resembled a giant musical box.

In autumn, at full harvest, all the villagers came and filled their baskets with the juicy fruits from which they made jams, herbal medicines and juices. They came in droves to hear the exquisite tunes played from these musical trees while they picked the plums. Students of Botany visited the castle as they tried to research more about the magic and mystery of the plum trees, but no science could explain their wonders.

Saffron loved to hear the cries of the small children as they played while the older folk collected the ripened fruit. But most of all she loved to stroke the wild animals that came in the cool evening to nibble and graze in the garden. They loved to be petted by the beautiful maiden. They knew that they would be safe from the hunts-men's roars, horns and yelping dogs in the safety of the castle.

But all was soon to change with the arrival of a wicked lad from the local village, called Martial, who came to work in the castle. He arrived with great praise from the local people and soon befriended everybody at the castle and especially Saffron. He used to sit with her and tell her wild and wonderful tales of faraway lands and strange beasts. He brought her little insects and animals which he had rescued. She began to rely on Martial more and more.

Saffron's father was a frail old man and he was becoming more dependent on his only daughter each day to manage the running of the castle. Martial would have no problem ensuring that his wicked schemes could be fulfilled.

Saffron and her father were so trusting that the castle had little security, except for a huge iron gate at the end of the large tree-lined avenue, which was locked every night. Martial made a copy of the great key so that he could then gain entrance any time that he wished. He decided on a plan. He would steal into the grounds of the castle and dig up the musical plum trees and sell them to make a profit.

At the next full moon, Martial crept into the castle with an accomplice, a small weasel of a man, who could squeeze through the tightest space or climb over the highest wall. They brought a large cart dragged by an old donkey. They pulled and tugged and dug up all the plum trees and threw them on the cart. The poor silent trees offered little resistance.

As their proud roots were torn from the ground, the plum trees' fruits would, from then on, remain silent. The donkey could barely pull the cart with the enormous load of heavy trees. Martial took the trees to the owner of a vast nursery in a big bustling town, praising their wondrous musicality. However, the owner had already heard the marvellous sounds when he used to pick fruit in season at Plum Tree Castle. There the trees stood in giant earthenware pots. People everywhere had heard about the famous musical plum trees.

The new owner of the trees could not wait to show off the musical power of the trees to the people. He would ask the Mayor to have the honour of plucking a plum from one tree, in front of a large crowd. The largest tree was put on show in the market in a giant golden tub.

One day, the Mayor, dressed in a long scarlet coat and golden chain, strutted along the red carpet laid down in his honour in the market place. If the Mayor liked what he saw, he would buy some of these wonderful fruit trees. He would place them all around the town for the benefit of the people.

The drums began to roll. The Mayor mopped his brow in the hot noonday sun and welcomed everyone. He then plucked the first plum, and everybody waited, spellbound. But alas, nothing happened. He plucked a second plum from the tree, and still nothing happened. He did it again, but no sound at all. The crowd was silent too.

Finally, in his exasperation, the Mayor started to pick and pluck from other trees in the hope of hearing some faint

sound from them, but alas nothing! All was silent around the trees, which stood under the hot sun without a flicker of their leaves. The Mayor was aghast. He felt such a fool in front of the people. They began to whisper among themselves. The buyer of the trees scratched his head. What was he to do? He had been swindled by that thief, Martial. He stammered and tried to explain to the Mayor.

"Mr Mayor, I really don't understand. When I went to the garden where these trees were growing, I heard the wonderful music when the plum trees were plucked. I do not know what has happened. I have been tricked."

"*You* have been tricked!" shrieked the Mayor. "How do you think *I* feel, you stupid little man, gathering all of the townspeople together, away from their work to watch this farce. A great spectacle indeed! You have been duped by swindlers, bigger fool you!" The Mayor then turned to the people.

"There has been a terrible mistake, please go back to your homes and places of work, there has been some misunderstanding. I am truly sorry."

So the crowd all dispersed, dragging their few belongings with them and sharing their disappointment. Some spat at the trees and others kicked them. The people did not know if they would ever trust the Mayor and his foolish schemes again.

Meanwhile, back at the castle, Martial was nowhere to be found. Now that he had the money from the sale of the trees, he had absconded. Saffron and her father were devastated when they discovered that all of the plum trees had been uprooted from their beloved garden.

"Oh, my darling trees, where are you? Who could have possibly taken you from your beloved home?" Saffron wept with sadness.

The wild fawns and other animals knew what had taken place and laid their tearful heads on Saffron's lap for comfort. Saffron cried with her father.

"Papa, we heard nothing, but they must have come during the night. With the full moon they would have been able to carry out their dreadful deed. It must have been somebody who knew the place. But who was able to open the gate? I'll ask Martial – he surely will help." But Saffron feared the worst.

Time passed, and the nursery owner managed to get rid of the fruit trees. They were placed in a large dump waiting to be burnt on a large autumn bonfire. Not only had they produced no music, but since being removed from the grounds of the castle, they bore only dry, withered plums. The Mayor wanted them out of sight as quickly as possible. Their very presence in the town reminded him of his foolhardiness. So the poor trees were destined for the scrap heap. They awaited their fate, when they would be set alight on a huge pyre and would be no more.

Shortly after this episode, Joseph, a student of botany at the university, visited the town with some fellow students, as he had heard about the theft of the famous plum trees and he was anxious to find out what had happened. Joseph had visited Plum Tree Castle before and had done some research into these amazing trees and their music. He was perplexed, like many others, as to the trees' marvellous ability to create such wonderful melodies.

He watched all the jugglers and acrobats performing in the open air at the fair before the famous lighting of the huge bonfire, but he was on a serious mission that night. They walked over to the great pyre, and there, on top of the huge pile, Joseph saw the famous plum trees. He was aghast at what he saw.

"Oh, poor plum trees, how sad that you are sitting on the pyre, awaiting the dreaded spark. I can't let this happen!" He ran immediately to get some help. However, as he ran back he could see the Mayor and his party approaching with lighted torches to set the pyre ablaze. He stopped the Mayor.

"Please, Mr Mayor, may I take the plum trees from the pyre? I believe that they were stolen from the famous Plum Tree Castle in a small village not far from here." The Mayor stopped and looked quizzically at the young student.

"Plum trees, indeed, don't mention these wretched trees! I have made a fool of myself in front of the entire village because of them. Such nonsense, musical trees indeed! I never heard such incredible stories. I can't wait to set the whole lot ablaze. Now out of my way, young man. We have work to do." With that he motioned to the torch-bearers. But Joseph was not deterred and stood in his path.

"Mr Mayor, these are famous trees and they were stolen. They are quite unique. I beg you to please let me take them away from here and plant them back into the ground of Plum Tree Castle, and I believe that they will sing again. You see, I am a student of botany, and I have been studying these wonderful trees. But we must be quick, as the trees will die shortly if they are not given water."

The Mayor looked at this young student, who was clearly distraught and spoke in a very passionate way about the plum trees. The Mayor was a kind man. His huffing and puffing and shouting were only his way of commanding attention. He felt that there could possibly be a grain of truth in the pleadings of this young bright man. He admired the youth's sincerity and passion.

"They will die with the spark from one of these torches young man, unless I change my mind. Now let me see what you are suggesting. You are of the opinion that if these trees are removed from here and placed back into the ground of Plum Tree Castle, they will sing again. Oh, I don't know, it all seems a bit of a tale to me. But I am prepared to give you a chance to prove your case."

The Mayor rubbed his brow with a handkerchief. He motioned to the torch-bearers, who withdrew for a while.

"Take the trees away at once but hurry as we need to light the bonfire," he said to Joseph.

"Be quick, young man, we have not all night. I don't hold much hope – the trees must be almost all dead at this stage. It will take a river of water to bring them back to life, but good luck."

Joseph shouted to his fellow students.

"Come on. We need strong hands and buckets and buckets of water. Quick, before it's too late or the trees will die."

The students rushed over to the great pyramid of wood and rubbish assembled for burning and quickly climbed and clambered up the bonfire. One by one they patiently removed the dry, tired plum trees until none were left. The Mayor and his party stood by watching Joseph and his fellow students. They then placed the fragile trees on a cart and got ready to make their way back to Plum Tree Castle.

"The trees have little time. The sap is dry and they need water and nourishment fast. We need strong oxen to take them back on the cart. Quick, waste no time!" Joseph shouted, and soon the cart was prepared and on its way. Two strong brown oxen bulls pulled the cart slowly

throughout the night in the full light of the moon. They stopped at an inn for some food and water for the bulls. As the sun came up, they slowly made their way up the great avenue of Plum Tree Castle.

The trees were almost dead as they were much withered

at this stage. They desperately needed to be replaced back into the earth.

All this time, Saffron and her papa had remained sad and forlorn since the theft of the plum trees. But she cheered up when she saw the two lovely strong bulls standing in the courtyard and the students unloading the trees.

"Oh, my beautiful trees, but is it too late? Will they play music again?"

"We must plant them immediately back into the earth," Joseph said. Then he spoke to his students, who were busy taking each tree gently from the cart.

"Waste no time, and prepare the earth immediately for the return of the plum trees and give them plenty of water."

When the trees were safely back in the freshly dug earth, Joseph turned to Saffron in the evening light and said, "We must await the summer when the plum trees will ripen and produce the musical fruits."

Saffron was so overjoyed that she took his hands in hers.

"I can't thank you enough for what you've done. You have no idea how sad my father and I were when we found out that our beloved trees had been taken so cruelly from this sacred soil," she sobbed.

Joseph was so taken with her plight that he bent down and kissed her hand.

"Saffron, it grieved me terribly when I heard what had happened to the trees. I couldn't bear to think of you here with your father without them, so that is why I wanted to restore them to you and plant them back in this sacred earth in the castle. Fear not. I promise you that the trees will recover and produce music, with kindness and good care. Please trust me."

So all through the winter Saffron and the creatures of the wild nourished the trees, watering and protecting their blossoms from the harsh winter frosts. Then at last summer came but Saffron was fearful that they would no longer produce the music. Then she remembered Joseph's promise and smiled.

As soon as the sun was at its highest in the sky and all around was in bloom, Saffron went out and placed her hand on a plum. She was nervous and held her breath as she plucked the first fruit. All of a sudden, the garden was filled with the chimes of sweet music. So overjoyed was Saffron that she hugged the tree and wheeled her chair in to tell her father, while clutching the plum.

"Oh, Papa, the fruit trees are producing their music like of old. I am so happy," she cried with joy. Her father, who was frail now, lifted his head and had tears in his eyes as she held the fruit aloft.

"My dear, it's a miracle, and we must thank that dear boy, Joseph. Now your dear mother can rest in her grave," and he hugged his daughter.

Meanwhile, Martial returned home after several months, having squandered all the money he had made from the sale of the plum trees on fine clothes, gambling, eating and drinking like a prince. He came back to his poor family full of swagger and boastfulness. He talked of how he had travelled the world climbing the great mountains, riding and taming wild horses and swimming in turbulent seas. His parents were happy to see him but did not trust him. People whispered in the village that it was he who had stolen the plum trees, as he had vanished the night they were stolen. Martial dismissed such rumours with a wave of his hand.

"Oh, it was all hearsay and rumour. Just a coincidence."

His mother was not deceived and replied, "The plum trees were returned by a kindly young student and are now still playing music, despite all that they had been through. Saffron and her father are ever so happy that they're back. It was a terrible shame on whoever carried out this terrible act on that poor girl and her frail father."

Martial was surprised when he heard this. "What do you mean the trees have been returned?"

His mother looked at him suspiciously. "Son, are you sure that you are telling me the truth? You have not been able to account for all the money you have recently acquired. Oh, look at you! All that finery and big talk. Your father is worried sick about you. We did not raise you for this."

Martial was silent. His mother knew him too well. Nobody in the village wanted to hire him for work, as they were suspicious that it was he who had stolen the precious trees from Saffron and her father. People walked on the other side of the street when he passed them in his fine clothes, so disgusted were they at his wicked behaviour.

One day while Joseph and some other students were visiting Plum Tree Castle, Martial paid Saffron a visit. The students were carrying out some research on the soil. Saffron greeted him warmly.

"Oh, Martial, are you well? I believe that you have been away for some time!"

Gallantly, Martial took her hand and kissed it. "Quite well, my lady. I trust that all is well with you and your father?"

Saffron told him about the plum trees and how they were returned thanks to Joseph. They strolled through the garden, and Saffron introduced Martial to Joseph. Then Saffron took Martial's arm and said, "Pluck a plum, just like old time's sake, and listen to the sweet music."

Martial approached a tree and plucked a plum, but instead of the beautiful musical sounds which would normally come from the picked fruit, there was silence. No music came forth from the tree. Instead the fruit which he held in his palm turned into a dirty green slimy mess. He tried another and another but no music was forthcoming. Joseph, who had been watching nearby, came over.

"Allow me to pick a fruit and listen to the music," Joseph said as he picked a fruit. The music flowed through the orchard. It was then that they realised that Martial had been the thief and that the rumours about him were all true. Joseph turned to Martial and said angrily, "You see, it is only from the sacred ground of the castle, where Caroline's grave lay, that the earth produced the fine musical sounds from the plum trees. Once the trees are ripped from the castle's soil they will remain silent for ever."

Martial stood quite still, as Joseph continued.

"Be off with you, you thieving scoundrel. You have no reason to be here. It was you who stole the trees and caused undue hardship and stress to this poor girl and her frail father."

Martial withdrew and left the grounds of Plum Tree Castle. He was driven out of the village and never returned. Joseph and Saffron became the best of friends and they both enjoyed the flowering plums and music from the trees for many years to come.

Sunflower

Sunflower the pony was very sick, as he had acquired an infection. He belonged to three small children: Marianne, Anthony and Brian.

"Please, please, Sunflower, take another sip, just one more, please," pleaded Marianne with tears in her eyes, as she offered him some warm water in a bowl, but he bowed his head and closed his eyes. He was too poorly to take even a sip of water.

"Oh, please get better, Sunflower," wept Brian, as he snuggled up to the sick pony. The children rubbed down Sunflower's hot sweaty coat with cold sponges to try and bring his fever down, but it was no use. They had wet his hay to improve his allergy, as the vet told them that dry hay was the cause of his condition. The little pony was indeed gravely ill.

"Sunflower needs expensive medicine from the vet to clear up that chest infection and make him better, but we can't afford another vet bill," murmured the children's father to a farmer, at the Christmas fair in the local village. The children wondered how they could collect money to buy the medicine to cure Sunflower. Then there were the scans and x-rays that had to be paid for. They had to buy fresh wet hay to ensure that their pony's allergy improved. The children thought of all sorts of things that they could do to collect money for Sunflower's recovery. It was coming up to Christmas, a festive time for all.

"I've a great idea," chirped Anthony.

"Not another of your crazy ideas," said Brian flicking a piece of rolled up paper at him. "Why don't we sing for him?" declared Anthony jumping up suddenly from his chair and waving his arms about.

"I think that's a wonderful idea," piped up Marianne.

So it was agreed that the three of them would sing for Sunflower.

"You can take the little cart from the shed and decorate it with a few streamers and some tinsel. Place the bucket for the money inside it, and wheel it into the centre of the city.

There'll be lots of people doing their Christmas shopping, and they'll all give generously," their mother told them as she said goodnight to them. Their mother spoke with such authority that the children rarely doubted her.

The children lived in a small house, not far from the city, so each day they took the bus to the big city with their little cart and bucket to sing for Sunflower. They placed the cart not far from a great big Christmas tree, decked with streamers, candles, ribbons and bells.

Each night, after collecting a few miserable pence, the children wheeled their cart along the busy streets of shoppers and headed home by bus.

"I'm a bit embarrassed with our small dull cart beside that magnificent tree," grumbled Brian.

"Oh, well, all we can do is to do our best for Sunflower and trust that people will give generously," said Marianne ringing her hands.

The small cart hated being beside the magnificent tree and would have preferred to be back in the farmyard, where at least it had felt very useful.

"I don't know why the children chose you, you miserable little cart. Look at your pathetic brown rusty handles and your rickety little wheels. You should be thrown on the scrap heap!" a passing seagull sneered down at him.

People came to listen to the choristers singing under the great Christmas tree. The various choirs and musicians collected a lot of money over Christmas, thereby helping their favourite charities, but the shoppers just passed the children by, with their plain soft voices, rattling their plastic bucket beside the little rusty cart.

Sunflower was not getting any better. In fact the poor pony was at death's door. He just held his head low most of the time, but occasionally gave them a sad, winsome look. Marianne tried to get him to breathe through his nebuliser, which helped his breathing, but it was no use. Sunflower was simply too weak. The children were frantic. They all knew that their world would stop if anything happened to Sunflower, whom they had tended and cared for since he was only six months old. He was part of this poor family. Now he was very weak and his breathing shallow. He had a nasty hollow cough. The children kept him warm in the little hut at the bottom of their tiny garden with straw and old blankets, but he seemed to be drifting further and further from them.

They desperately needed to have the money to pay for the expensive medicine which would make him better, but time was running out for all of them. Just two days before Christmas, at the height of the shopping spree, the children had only collected half of the money required to buy the medicine to save Sunflower's life. They were worried as to what might happen to their pet pony over Christmas. That evening, having sung till near exhaustion, the children were so anxious to get home to check on Sunflower that in their haste they forgot to take the cart with them. It remained beside the Christmas tree shivering on its little rusty wheels. The wind howled around it, toppling it over on its side. A young boy kicked its frail handles, hurtling it up against the railings. Shaking some dew from the tree's boughs, the tree muttered "Miserable little thing!" An old beggar man lay on the ground under the tree with his few rags and tried to keep warm by snuggling under his torn duvet.

People passed by and barely looked at the small pathetic cart. There it lay, as insignificant as the Christmas tree was magnificent. Mr MacDaragh, the city , made his rounds every night in his special green glass box, which moved on silver wheels. The magician remained inside the

glass box, preparing potions and conjuring up tricks and spells. He was a kind soul, always helping people and trying to make things better for everyone. He wore a long black and mauve cloak made of the finest silk, with a diamond seam around the edge which dazzled and glowed in the midnight light. His glittering hat was scattered with precious stones of red, blue and green. No one could see inside the box, but the great magician could see everything that went on outside.

"Good evening, Christmas tree. What a lovely sight you are in this city," the clever magician said, poking his head out of the box. The tall tree preened itself and rattled its bells and baubles with excitement. Then the magician spied the poor miserable cart on its side, near the railings.

"Oh dear. I must do something about this," he said, as he jumped out of his magic glass box.

"Poor little cart, I know all about you. You see, a wise magician knows everything. I see all things. Would you like to be a beautiful cart?" As the wind howled around him, the little cart looked curiously at the magician.

"Yes, but I am plain and miserable and nobody is interested in me," the cart stammered.

Smiling at him, Mr MacDaragh held one of the cart's rusty handles in his magician's hand and said, "I shall make you into a fine handsome carriage that anyone would be proud to own."

The small cart was surprised and wondered why anyone as clever as Mr MacDaragh would want to have anything to do with him. After all, he was just a plain old cart. "What do you mean?"

"Trust me, little one," the magician said placing a hand on his handles. Then he spilled some magic snow in a circular motion in the frosty night air. Looking up at the twinkling stars, he blew bubbles: pink ones to change the size of something, blue bubbles to change its shape and gold bubbles to make something more beautiful. All of a sudden the small cart rose up and a white glistening substance sparkled on it in the moonlight. The cart stood upright and was now transformed into a beautiful and elegant carriage, shimmering white against the pale glow of night. Its four shiny silver wheels, studded with tiny diamonds, no longer creaked, but instead moved around as smoothly as if turning on velvet. Its little red handles shone like rubies in the snow. Inside, the tin cup changed into a magnificent white marble bowl.

The magician placed fifty long silver plumes in the cart. Whoever would write with these plumes writes in silver ink, in a rare and beautiful script.

A great change had taken place. Instead of being shy

and timid, the cart stood proudly in its new shape, as a glistening great white carriage, almost twice the size of the little cart. The Christmas tree was aghast at this change and turned away in disgust, pretending not to notice the dazzling carriage beside her.

"What cheek to change into something you're not! I suppose in the morning you'll return to being the miserable, horrible little cart that you really are," the tree uttered, firmly shaking her boughs in disgust.

In the morning the children were downcast as they walked slowly to their place beside the majestic Christmas tree with heads bent low. They were very sad, as Sunflower was very, very poorly. This was their last day to sing for his medicine. Suddenly they saw the change which had taken place. Instead of a grotty and rusty little cart falling apart, they saw a sparkling white carriage in the frosty morning, with shiny red handles. Clearly overjoyed, they cried, "Oh where's our little cart? What has happened?"

The old beggar moved under his ragged mattress and glared at the children.

"That's your cart. The magician was here last night and he did all sorts of magic and changed your cart into this wonderful carriage which you see before you."

Marianne lifted up one of the long silver plumes.

"What a beautiful feather! But what are we to do with them? Are they ours to keep?"

The scruffy man rose to his feet and wiped the dust off his ragged clothes.

"Indeed they are yours to do as you like. Oh, those

plumes are very rare. Whoever writes with them will write a magnificent script in silver, just like the scribes of old. The magician placed them in the cart. He was a kindly old soul. You'll get good money for those feathers and then you can help your little pony to get better." The children wondered about the old man and how he could know so much about the magician and his plumes. He seemed well-spoken despite his rags.

"Come on, let's sing for all our worth with this beautiful white carriage for Sunflower," Brian cried. Up until now, people had been too busy to notice the poor children. Now everybody stopped to admire the beautiful carriage, which spangled like pearl drops in the winter's sun. People asked the children why they were collecting money, and when they heard about Sunflower and how poorly he was, they gave generously. People were enchanted with the silver plumes. Soon the plumes were all sold, and the children had nearly collected all the money for Sunflower.

Late that afternoon when everyone was weary with shopping and rushing around to buy the last-minute trimmings for Christmas, a smart lady came rushing by with lots of shopping bags. She was holding a little girl, called Aoife, by the hand.

"Mummy, Mummy, look at the beautiful carriage," Aoife called. The lady was in a frantic state, as they had not yet bought a Christmas tree for their home, and most of the Christmas trees had been sold. However, the little girl had clearly fallen for the lovely white carriage and refused to follow her mother.

"Come now, darling, we have no time to linger," the mother cried, dragging the child away. But Aoife refused to move, so taken was she with the carriage.

"Mummy, Mummy, please, look at the beautiful little carriage!"

"Why indeed, it is pretty," the lady murmured. Then she noticed the children and how eager they were to collect money.

"Hello, children. What are you collecting for?" the lady enquired.

"Please can you help us? We only need a small amount of money to buy the medicine for our sick pony. We have collected a lot of money, but we are still short!" Anthony cried. The lady took pity on them.

"Oh, you poor darlings. Aren't you wonderful children and so kind to do this for your little pony? He must be a very, very special pony," she said.

"There is no pony like him in the whole world," sobbed Brian.

"Well, in that case, I would like to buy the carriage from you for my little girl here. I'll give a very generous sum for it, with some extra money for yourselves to get some Christmas presents and of course to pay for your darling pony's medicine. It would look lovely in the hallway of our home."

"We hate selling our lovely little cart, but we desperately need the money for our sick pony," sobbed Marianne. The children were sad to say goodbye to their little cart, which had brought them so much luck, but they would do anything to save Sunflower's life. Without this money, Sunflower would surely die that night.

"Thank you, thank you so much for helping us," Anthony said as he gave Aoife a kiss on the cheek.

"Goodbye, little cart, and good luck," the children shouted as they ran off to get the bus to take them home to buy medicine to save Sunflower.

Back at the children's house, the vet was already there and looked at Sunflower gravely. He shook his head a number of times as he examined the poor sick pony. Their mother was frightened, as things appeared to be gloomy, and she was dreading what she would have to tell the children, and so near to Christmas. She felt that this bad news would break their little hearts. Then she heard them shouting and laughing outside.

"We've got the money to save Sunflower!" the children cried, as they burst into the hut. They stopped as they saw their mother's sad face, and then they noticed the vet standing there with a grave look in his eyes.

"You have very little time, children, to save your pony, but if you go down to the pharmacy as quick as you can and get this medicine for him, you might have a chance. It might be too late, of course. Don't delay. Go at once, as Sunflower is failing fast. I have spoken to your father and have given the pony an injection which might help to fight the infection, but he needs to continue with his medicine and nebuliser," the vet advised.

Anthony sped down to the chemist on his bike and was just in time before it closed for Christmas. He bought the drugs that the vet had prescribed and that night Sunflower started on his medicine. The children took it in turns to stay up with him all night. Marianne brushed down his damp coat to keep his fever at bay. By dawn he had improved slightly and by midday the weak little pony was able to take small sips of water. Marianne wrapped her arms around him and buried her face in his mane and cried with happiness.

"Oh Sunflower, I would be so, so sad if anything happened to you," she sobbed into his soft coat.

The children danced around their little pony and sang songs of joy. Their mother had knit Sunflower a soft woolly scarf to keep him warm and placed hot water bottles around his bed on Christmas Day. The children fed him with warm drinks. Soon he opened his soft eyes as if to say, "Thank you, children."

A few days after Christmas, Sunflower was able to stand on his wobbly legs and by New Year's Day the children led him out for a small walk. They were as proud of their little pony as he walked out with his shiny bridle adorned with ivy and berries. His lovely light brown coat glowed as the children showed him off to all of their friends.

"Three cheers for Sunflower, who is getting better and will be well again soon!" they cried with joy.

Meanwhile the small white carriage was placed in the hallway of the lady and Aoife's house and awaited the arrival of Santa Claus. After Christmas all the little girl's friends visited the house and opened their presents around it.

"I think that our little white carriage is much prettier than a big Christmas tree," Aoife said proudly. People from the neighbourhood came to admire the beautiful white carriage, as they had not seen anything as pretty for such a long time.

"Why, it is absolutely magnificent and so unusual, we have never seen the like before," they said.

"And you are unlikely to see the like again," the little girl's mother said puffing out her chest and straightening up. Each night the children danced and sang songs around it. When Christmas was over the beautiful white carriage was taken upstairs to the little girl's bedroom, where it stayed for many years.

Sunflower got better and gave all of the children in the village rides on his back. His beautiful glossy mane shone like it had before his illness, and his eyes sparkled. Within a few weeks he was pulling the children in a sleigh up and down the quiet roads, as happy as any other little pony. As the months passed, Sunflower grew strong and healthy again.

Every year, at Christmas time, Anthony, Marianne and Brian visit the city, and as they walk down the main street they think of their little cart and their heroic efforts which saved Sunflower's life, and they smile with happiness.

But what the children never knew was that the kindly old man on the street used to turn himself into the magician Mr MacDaragh during the night, to do good deeds and to help those in distress. Once dawn came up, he changed back to the old scruffy man observing and watching out for all those who needed help.

The Ballerina

Water's Edge, a great house, stood majestically overlooking a lake. It nestled among magnificent trees on the edge of a wood. Flossie, a frail elderly lady, lived there with her Siamese cat, Kim. Apart from her daughter, Greta, she rarely had visitors.

Although cold and damp, Water's Edge was a charming place. A grand piano stood in a finely furnished room where the sun beamed through its large bay window. Delicate figurines stood on the piano, including a graceful ballerina made of the finest porcelain. Flossie called the little dancer Lisa, and Lisa had been part of this family for generations. She had been created in the great Meissen porcelain factory in Berlin in 1762. The wafer-thin porcelain folds of Lisa's ballet dress were of the faintest pink colour. A crown of cream rosebuds perched on her golden hair, which was studded with tiny blue diamonds, matching her eyes, which were as blue as the wild forget-me-nots that grew everywhere in the woods around Water's Edge.

Lisa looked as if she were ready to perform a pirouette. People admired the delicate little ballet dancer, but Lisa did not like being handled by different visitors. She grew tired, too, of Kim's regular trots along the top of the piano among the ornaments to chase a spider or swipe at a hanging cobweb. But most of all she desired to dance, and dance the whole night long.

One night, as Flossie and Kim slept soundly in the house and the moon's brightness created dazzling shadows around the room, Lisa decided to fulfil a dream she harboured. She sprang off the piano and performed pirouettes, arabesques and free spins, gliding up and down the polished piano wood, dancing like she had never danced before. Springing onto the mantelpiece, she grabbed the grumpy old Toby Jugs and jived with them, while the crystal clock chimed away to its heart's content.

She whirled around the silver-framed photographs and glided among the silver pieces. The stern ladies and gentlemen of the family portraits looked disapprovingly at the little ballet dancer as she perched on their gilded frames. Finally, exhausted after all the dancing, she dived into the crystal vase of cool spring water, containing fresh wild roses. But then, like a trapeze artist, she swung onto the rich green curtains, climbing up the smooth velvet like a frisky kitten to perch on the pole holding up the magnificent drapes. Kim watched in amazement as the little ballerina performed her dances and dreamt of inviting some of the local cats to partake in the fun too.

Lisa never made a sound and by morning she returned to her home on top of the piano, ready to be brushed with a large ostrich feather duster by the cleaner.

Every evening, when all was hushed, Lisa would emerge from her position on the piano and dance the nights away.

One night, when all was quiet in the house, Lisa heard sounds in the kitchen, followed by whispers. Two men were moving around, and they had a torch. They came into the room with the piano and removed the paintings off the walls and helped themselves to the silver on the small cabinet by the window. Lisa lay quite still until a rough black-gloved hand grabbed her, tightly rolled her up in bubble wrap to prevent her from breaking and shoved her into a smelly old sack, along with other pieces of china and silver.

The thieves worked stealthily and methodically, removing everything from the room except the piano and a few chairs. They made off on foot out into the cold night air. They shoved Lisa and the other priceless objects away in a damp warehouse. She was passed around until she finally ended up at an auction room. Before the auction started, people lifted her up and admired her.

A finely dressed man who bought and sold precious objects sauntered into the auction house. He picked up Lisa and studied her carefully.

"Lovely piece of porcelain," he muttered to himself and moved on. The auction started, and everybody took their seats. After hours of bidding, Lisa's turn came. She was nervous, and she felt cold. She could hear the buzz of excitement in the audience when the auctioneer with his great booming voice held her aloft for all to see.

"Ah, here we have a fine piece, a little jewel, one of the rarest figures here today." People started to call out their

bidding prices and stick up their hands or catalogues to make a bid. Finally the auctioneer banged his gavel on the desk and roared at the audience, "Going, going, gone to the gentleman in the second row!"

The little ballet dancer was taken to an old shop out in the country. There she was placed with china tea sets and dinner services and stacks of boring pale lemon plates, some even cracked. The shop smelled of wet hay. She missed the fine grand piano in Flossie's house and often wondered what had become of the dear old lady. How she longed to see her again and to see the broad smile of the cleaner as she glided the ostrich feathers over Lisa's face and legs. How she longed for a rub of Kim's long sleek elegant tail, as the cat curled her way through the figurines on the piano.

A grubby price tag was tied tightly around her ankle. Lisa remained in this dreary place for months. She cried to herself each night and longed to dance, but could not because of the horrid heavy price tag tied tightly around her leg. She dared not anyway in these cold lifeless surrounds. Besides there was no piece which looked remotely interesting. She simply could not imagine dancing with a side plate!

One afternoon a young lady dropped by. She looked as if she had been hiking in the mountains as she was wearing big heavy boots and rainwear. About to leave, her eye spied the little ballet dancer who was hidden behind an ugly red and gold chipped vase.

Picking Lisa up, the lady looked at her carefully.

"I've seen this little piece somewhere before. But where, I wonder? She's simply exquisite. I know just the person who would love to have her," she murmured. Handling her gently, she enquired as to the origin of the little figurine, but the owner shrugged his shoulders and muttered, "Oh, I go to so many auctions, it's just one of many purchases… I really could not say, but it's a nice little piece and I dare say quite valuable."

"Please, please, buy me," Lisa cried silently to herself as she was being handled. The lady looked at the price tag, bargained with the old man, and agreed a price. Lisa wished with all her heart to leave that dreary dull shop, miles from anywhere, with little excitement except for a trickle of day-trippers on a Sunday afternoon.

The old man wrapped Lisa in brown paper and handed her to the lady. When the lady arrived home she lifted Lisa carefully from the paper and wrapped her gently in thin sheets of pink tissue paper. She then placed her in a comfortable box, smelling of beautiful spring flowers.

"Greta will be thrilled with this little figurine, oh, I know she will," the lady said excitedly.

For weeks Lisa lay silently in the dark folds of paper with the scent of flowers in the tiny box. However, she could still hear the faint sound of laughter, and sometimes, on a clear day, she could hear birdsong in the garden.

One day the wrapping was removed, and Lisa finally saw the bright light after weeks in the dark. Gentle hands held her.

"Why, it's Lisa! No it can't be – long-lost little Lisa. I can't believe it!" Greta was so excited that she kissed the little ballerina and held her closely.

"Oh, Mum will be so happy to know that we have found Lisa again," she sobbed heartily.

The little ballerina was returned to her rightful place on the piano at Water's Edge. Flossie was thrilled to have Lisa back again.

"Oh I know we shouldn't get too attached to ornaments. After all, they are not like people, but Lisa is special, and when she disappeared...well, I felt as if a little piece of my own heart was missing. It is amazing that she was found and ended up back at Water's Edge, where she truly belongs," Flossie said to Greta, holding back the tears.

Greta, who loved her mother dearly and would do anything for her, looked at Lisa and then her mother.

"Mum, I knew that Lisa meant so much to you, after all, she had belonged to grand-pappy. I had hoped with all my heart one day to find her, and I am so glad that we did," Greta said, giving her mother a big hug.

"Yes, indeed. With Lisa gone, I felt that some of my past had disappeared too," her mother said, drying away a tear.

The other pieces, with whom Lisa used to dance the night away, were gone forever from Water's Edge. But Kim was still there bounding and leaping after every insect and cobweb. Lisa proudly remains to this day on the top of the grand piano, where she still dances every night to her heart's content.

The Coral Queen

The city council was looking for a magnificent boat to celebrate the 1000th birthday of their great city. The council members searched all along the coast until they came upon a stately vessel which had been moored in a harbour some miles away. She was a fine majestic boat, painted blue and white with a great tall golden mast and billowing yellow sails. She was called the *Coral Queen*. She was so tall, towering over all other boats in the harbour, that she could see

images of the entire coastline. She was the envy of all the other boats. Her mast soared like a huge spear in the sky. But she was a proud boat, whose stateliness had caused her to become haughty and intolerant. Her behaviour earned her much envy from the other boats in the small harbour.

The council chose the *Coral Queen* to celebrate the city's 1000th birthday. The city had a proud sea-faring history for many years.

The *Coral Queen* waved goodbye to all the other boats in the bay with her great big sails, many of whom were glad to see her go, as they were tired of her endless bragging.

She was sad to leave the little harbour, where she had reigned supreme, but was looking forward to the admiration that she would receive from the passers-by in the city, with all the fuss and pomp of the great city's birthday celebration. She used to boast how she could see as far as the mountains across the sea on a clear day, such was her height, when all the other boats jostled and shook their sails to try and see beyond the horizon.

The *Coral Queen* was transported on a huge lorry to the centre of the city. The magnificent boat was moored on the river in the centre of the city. She was covered with strands of lights, not yet lit, waxen candles, silver baubles, red velvet bows and gold streamers. She looked truly wonderful. However, she was surrounded by much taller buildings. No longer could she see the coastline and her beloved sea. Still, she was happy with the fuss and publicity surrounding Christmas and didn't miss her natural surroundings.

Soon the Lord Mayor of the city and other dignitaries arrived in a beautiful glass coach to light up the great boat. Photographers clicked their cameras around the proud boat, and the Lord Mayor made a speech before switching on the Christmas lights. Suddenly the boat was aglow with light. Children assembled around its base and started to sing carols, and then the whole place lit up with brightness and song. *Coral Queen* was so excited, as she had never known such attention. She thought that she was a very lucky boat indeed.

On New Year's Day, *Coral Queen* was the centre of attention to celebrate the city's 1000th birthday. Dignitaries and royalty arrived, and the president of the country stepped on board and broke a bottle of champagne on her proud mast to celebrate a new era. It truly was a grand time for the magnificent and proud boat. Her photographs appeared in newspapers far and wide. But, sadly, in life, all good things come to an end.

After the celebrations, all was bleak. The streets in the city were bereft of life and a cold gloom descended on the place. *Coral Queen* felt lonely, as there was nobody around to admire her. By the end of the week people damaged her fine mast while trying to climb to her top. Empty bottles and cans were strewn around her once proud deck. She looked very glum and miserable.

"I hate it here. I wish I were back reigning supreme in the harbour once more," she sighed one windy evening, as her sails shook in the shrill gusts. Her mast rattled in fury. A wise old woman, who was also a soothsayer, hobbled up to the *Coral Queen* and stood in front of her, waving her stick.

"*Coral Queen*. You have been vain and haughty, and your snobbery will be your downfall. You should learn to be humble and kind to all, even to the most miserable of things. Be gone now from the city, and wherever you go, remember that life is not all about cameras and photo shoots. It is about having respect and cherishing all." She turned and hobbled off, leaving the *Coral Queen* in a more confused state than ever.

Soon men from the City Corporation came and took the boat away. They stripped her of her lights and fine ribbons. *Coral Queen* thought that she was going somewhere else with more lights, decorations and ribbon. How wrong she was!

Her owner had become old and tired and could no longer afford to look after her. She returned to the small harbour. While she was still a fine boat, she needed new equipment but this was very costly.

So the grand boat remained in the harbour, watching all of the other fishing boats sail out in the wind and stormy seas, returning laden with huge catches of fish. She hated to see the other boats full of life, either taking groups out deep sea fishing or else hosting parties on board in the long summer evenings. How she longed for joy and company and fulfilment.

Her paint began to peel off, and after a while, even her once proud name, *Coral Queen*, was no longer legible on her side, as it had eroded with the salt sea breezes.

One winter's day during a great storm, a father and his two sons had gone out fishing and had not returned. Days went by and the men made no contact with their families. People were frantic and frightened and feared the worst. A group of fishermen and divers got together and decided to go in search of the men, as time was moving on. Each day brought more and more fear and worry to their families.

The fishermen decided to stop fishing for a while until the men were found, so all the boats were called in from their fishing expeditions to help search for the missing men. While shabby and neglected, the *Coral Queen* was still the strongest and sturdiest boat in the harbour. All her engines were functioning well despite her shabby state. The men rigged her up with ropes, radios, winches, thermal blankets and all that was necessary for the rescue and safe return of the father and his two sons.

A helicopter buzzed overhead out in the wide open sea,

as the *Coral Queen* ploughed bravely through the rough seas. On and on she strode; out into faraway treacherous waters, where monstrous waves lashed up against her bow. Her mast shook with the crash of the spume and slap of the great salty sea. One time she dipped into a trough of swirling water, surrounded by mountainous waves. She left the other boats behind in the search. Her crew thought they were doomed. But still the brave *Coral Queen* righted herself and battled on in the heaving tide.

Although the men on board used navigational equipment to plot out a route, the *Coral Queen* seemed to steer her own course. It was as if her mast could signal where the doomed and stricken men lay. On and on she ploughed, ducking and weaving in her own time, and following her own route, so much so that the skipper just let her continue. He had an eerie feeling that perhaps the *Coral Queen* was heading in the direction of the shipwreck. He called the men together.

"In shipwrecks like this, sometimes we don't know where to go or what path to follow, so let us be led by the *Coral Queen* or by some strange force and see what fate has in store for us. Be brave my men. Have confidence in me and in this great sturdy boat. She won't let us down," he said reassuringly, slapping her great mast. The men understood. They trusted their skipper who had brought them home safely through many a gale and storm.

After two days out at sea and as dusk descended, the skipper spied something in the distance. He called on his radio to the pilot in the helicopter.

"We've sighted something over to the east by the far rocks. It could possibly be a shipwreck." He then gave the helicopter pilot the *Coral Queen*'s precise location. Her crew steered her to the area where the wreck was sighted. They soon came across a small life-raft where three men clung beside the wreck of their fishing boat, which was slowly disintegrating with the force of the huge tide. Everywhere pieces of wood floated around them in the swirling tide, as waves lashed and smacked against the doomed shipwreck.

The *Coral Queen* moved closer to the stricken men. The helicopter positioned itself over the men in mid-air. The helicopter crew winched the men up one by one from the tiny raft and placed them safely onto the waiting *Coral Queen*. There the rescue team gave the frightened and weak men food, shelter and warmth and all that was necessary to keep them safe until their return to dry land.

The *Coral Queen* fearlessly sailed the treacherous seas that evening and brought the men safely home. Cheering crowds waved and celebrated their arrival as the brave boat and her crew made their way into the small harbour. A huge roar rose from the crowd, as the boat moored alongside the quays. A waiting ambulance took the men to a nearby hospital.

All of the men recovered and eventually were safely reunited with their families.

All the other boats in the harbour showed the *Coral Queen* the praise that was her due. They rattled their masts and shook their sails with admiration to show their approval of the heroic efforts she made to save the men. But the skipper and his crew knew that by some strange force it was the *Coral Queen* alone who steered them to the stricken shipwreck. Photographers came to take pictures of her and she was again the toast of all.

With time, her owner sold the *Coral Queen*. Now she transports tourists up and down the coast on short pleasure cruises as well as ferrying bird watchers and nature lovers to the local islands. But the *Coral Queen*'s great feat in rescuing the fishermen one cold winter's day is a secret the crew keep in their hearts and she will be remembered by all for years to come.

Lilly and Frankie

Lilly and Frankie were twins. They were rarely apart, even for a few minutes, as they did everything together. They were known as the 'terrible two', as their pranks were legendary. Lilly had fiery red hair, cropped short, with the most beautiful but mischievous green eyes. Frankie was athletic, with brown hair and was the same height as Lilly.

Their mother Patricia had almost given up on them.

The children had gone to Lorna Murray's birthday party and had taken their two pet mice, Minky and Molly, with them. Lilly phoned Patricia after a while from the party.

"Mum, guess what? Frankie has let Minky and Molly loose at the party."

"Oh no!" gasped Patricia.

"Mum, yes, and there's more. When Mrs Murray was cutting the birthday cake, the mice ran all over the place, in and out of the cakes and sandwiches. Everybody was screaming. One of the mice ended up swimming in the cream while the other is under an armchair."

"Oh for heaven's sake! I had better come over and sort

things out. Mrs Murray will be furious." Patricia slammed down the phone.

When Patricia arrived at the Murray's house she could hear shrieking and screaming inside. Children were rushing about wildly.

"There he is – over there! Look! I see him," someone yelled.

Mrs Murray opened the door with a thunderous face. Frankie and Lilly stood beside her with their coats in their arms, ready to leave.

"Hello Mum," Lilly said innocently, as if nothing had happened.

"I'm so sorry, Mrs Murray, about the children's behaviour. It won't happen again. I hope that this episode has not ruined Lorna's birthday party," Patricia stammered.

"It certainly won't happen again, because I won't be inviting these two monkeys to any more birthday parties here," Mrs Murray said, glaring down at the twins.

"And I hope that the cat gets those mice that are running wild inside," she added, folding her arms.

"I'm not leaving until they're found," declared Frankie and he sat down on the doorstep with a glum face. "May I go in please? I think I can catch the mice," Patricia said, as she swept past Mrs Murray and went into the room where she could see the children rushing around wildly and squealing. Frankie got up and he and Lilly trailed behind Patricia. Patricia knew that if anything were to happen to Minky and Molly her life would just be a misery. So the mice had to be found!

She clapped her hands. The children stopped their shrieking and running around and stood to attention.

"Girls and boys! We are going to try and catch the little mice, wherever they are. But you must be very quiet, otherwise they won't come out. They are much more frightened of you than you need be of them. But please, please, we must have silence," Patricia whispered, putting her finger to her lips.

The children stopped squealing and remained silent, while Patricia spoke. Patricia had brought some tiny pieces of cheese in her purse and knew how to entice Minky out. She gave the piece to Frankie who knelt down beside her. He stretched out a cupped hand with some cheese, and called out to the mouse.

"Minky, out you come. Come on, I know you're there," he whispered softly. Lilly was standing close by near the armchair. She knew that Molly would soon follow. The children all jostled up near the armchair to catch a glimpse of Minky.

After a few minutes, a little pink nose poked out from under the armchair.

The children screamed and yelled as Minky proceeded to sniff the air and smell the cheese. Frankie then reached out and swiftly lifted the frightened rodent up, placing it in his mother's handbag. They waited for Molly, but there was no sign of her, until one of the children let out a shriek, "Quick. There it is."

Lilly saw Molly scamper along the carpet near the window, and quick as a flash she rushed over and caught the frightened mouse by the tail before Molly had time to hide under the armchair or run up behind the thick curtain. The children were all giggling as Lilly placed the mouse in Patricia's handbag. Patricia and the twins were in the hall and ready to leave.

"Oh Lilly, don't go, please stay. We'll miss you both, and it's early yet. We still have all the games to play outside," pleaded Lorna holding onto Lilly.

"Mummy can we stay, please?" begged Lilly, as Patricia gathered up their coats.

"No, I think that's enough for today. Come on children," she said as they all trooped past a shocked Mrs Murray and out the front door.

Lorna stood in the hallway with tears in her eyes, as

her best friend Lilly would not share the rest of her birthday celebrations with her.

That evening back at home, their mother left the twins in the kitchen while she went upstairs.

"Bet you can't get your mashed potato to stick higher on the wall than mine," Lilly giggled, as she hurled a spoonful of creamy yellow mash, which hit the wall over a painting and started to melt and fall.

"Watch this," said Frankie, as he filled his fork with a heaped portion of gooey potato, which he flung and which landed a bit higher on the wall than Lilly's mash.

Soon the wall was covered in lumps of melting buttery potatoes, sliding down in great big blobs on to the floor. The wall looked like a moving mountain of mashed potato. The children giggled. Frankie juggled and caught his two sausages in the air. Suddenly their mother stood at the door carrying Lilly's tennis skirt.

"Lilly, how come your tennis skirt is dyed blue? And where did you get the blue dye? It's everywhere. You can't play tennis in a blue skirt," Patricia said, going over and frantically trying to wash the stain off the skirt under the tap. "I got it from the blue stuff to clean the lavatory. I hate wearing white," Lilly said with a grin. Patricia was about to leave when she saw the wall.

"What is that? What have you done? You promised me on the way home from the party that you would be good. You will clean up this mess at once and then go immediately up to bed. I've had more than enough for one day," she shouted at them, flinging the tennis skirt into the washing machine.

"But Mum, we were only—" Frankie tried to speak.

"Not a word. Clean and then upstairs!" their mother said as she furiously emptied their plates into the rubbish bin. The children knew that they were in trouble. After they had gathered up the soggy balls of mash from the floor, the twins slowly climbed the stairs to their bedroom. Their mother called after them.

"You'll get no pocket money and no treats for a week. I have decided that I am definitely going to send you two off to boarding school next term, as I simply can't look after you anymore. You are too badly behaved." Patricia leaned over the sink in the kitchen and started to sob. It was now the end of June and this meant that they would only have two more months of freedom before school.

As they brushed their teeth in the bathroom, Frankie said to Lilly, "I am not going away to any school, ever! I'll run away before that."

Lilly smudged the red and white toothpaste all over her lips and then squeezed the remainder of the toothpaste on the mirror, drawing a smiling face of a clown. Laughing at herself in the mirror, Lilly chuckled, "I won't either. So there."

Catching up Satsuma, her orange and brown guinea pig, to take to bed with her, Lilly sighed, "I've a great idea. Let's run away if Mum and Dad send us off to boarding school." Satsuma slept at the end of Lilly's bed every night.

The next day, their music teacher, Miss Lemon, arrived at the house for the twins' weekly piano lesson at 6 o'clock. Their mother had decided that it was easier for Miss Lemon to come to the house, so that the twins could be supervised during their lesson. They did not like Miss Lemon.

"I hate the way she looks at me over her glasses," Lilly said and Frankie agreed.

"She's like a seagull with her pointy nose and beady eyes that look right through me."

"She looks like an old witch," Lilly said doodling and

then drawing a cat on the cover of her music book.

Miss Lemon began to assemble her music books when the twins burst into the piano room at the end of the house.

"Hello, Miss Lemon!" they screamed together.

"Hello, children. I hope that you've been practising your pieces. The exams will be soon, and you must know all your scales," she said, peering at them over her spectacles.

Frankie went over and sat on the piano stool and started to play his scales. As he played, he thought of ways to get out of these piano lessons. He hated all the practice, and he didn't like the way Miss Lemon constantly found fault with him. Miss Lemon sat down on the chair beside him.

Suddenly she screamed and stood up.

"What is that?" she said helplessly, as a yellow sticky liquid started to flow onto her stockings and dripped onto her finest leather shoes.

Frankie suddenly remembered the six hens' eggs he had taken from the fridge and hidden under the cushion on Miss Lemon's chair. He had forgotten all about Miss Lemon and his piano lesson. He thought he had better tell the truth.

"Oh, Miss Lemon, I'm so sorry. I forgot that I had put the eggs there. Um, I was hiding them under the cushion to take them into school tomorrow for science class," he stammered. He couldn't tell her that the reason why he had taken the eggs was to pelt them at teasers such as Denny Hurley and Finny McCloskey.

Miss Lemon rushed from the room to get some paper towels and cloths to clean herself. Patricia met her in the corridor.

"What's the matter, Miss Lemon?" Patricia asked.

"Look at the state of my clothes and my new shoes!"

"Oh, I'm so sorry," exclaimed Patricia.

"And you should see your beautiful carpet!"

"What?" Patricia gasped.

"I've never taught such wild children. You need to do something about that pair, or somebody else will! Leaving raw eggs for people to sit on them like a clucking hen!" Miss Lemon said tearfully as she made her way to the kitchen.

The new beige carpet was covered in egg yolks that continued to drip from the stool. Frankie bent down and tried to clear away the eggshells and sticky yellow slime with his hands. Lilly was sitting on the nearby sofa giggling so hard that she thought she would burst.

"Oh my lord! I'll deal with you two in a minute. Do not move, either of you. Is that understood?" Patricia yelled at the pair, and then fled to the kitchen before Miss Lemon departed.

A few weeks after this episode, in July, they were all sitting in the kitchen playing some board games. The parents had decided that the twins would be sent away to boarding school at the end of the summer. "You'll be weekly boarders. When I went to boarding school we boarded in September and didn't come home again until

Christmas," Patricia said, trying to console them. She was firm and adamant that they were going off and she was not going to change her mind.

"Oh Mum, I promise that we'll be good. We'll even help you clean the house," stammered Lilly, clambering up on a chair and taking bits of Patricia's hair to plait.

"Mum, I promise to keep Minky and Molly up in the bedroom all the time and not let them out, please, please, Mum, don't send us away," Frankie sobbed as he got up from his chair and put his arms around his mother's waist. But Patricia was getting tired of the endless reasons the twins listed as to why they should not be sent away, not to mention all their promises of being forever well-behaved.

"Oh, Mum, we promise we'll be good. We'll never cause you any more trouble. Promise, promise," Frankie pleaded with his mother.

"No. That's final. My mind is made up. I simply can't go on apologising to everybody for your behaviour," their mother said, wrenching herself away from their grasps and going out to the garden to get some fresh air.

So, in the middle of August, the twins became nervous and dreaded the day when they would be parted from each other, to meet again only at the weekends.

"It's terrible that Mum and Dad are sending us away. I don't think they love us anymore," sobbed Lilly.

"Don't be such a baby, Lilly. That's not true. It's just that we're a little bit bolder than other kids. Maybe it's because we're twins," sighed Frankie, opening his book and getting ready for bed.

"I'm going to sleep and hope that I'll never wake up again, 'cause I don't want to go to boarding school," Lilly said, pulling up the bedclothes around her.

Frankie made his way out to his bedroom, which was next to Lilly's.

It was a balmy night, and all was quiet in the house. Satsuma lay asleep on Lilly's bed and was snoring peacefully. Patricia had gone to bed early, as their father was away for a few days playing golf. It was about 2am, and dark gloomy clouds hid the moonlight from the room.

Frankie woke suddenly when he heard a noise downstairs, like somebody rummaging. He tiptoed out of his bedroom and looked over the bannisters. He spied a light downstairs coming from what seemed to be a torch. He then went and put on his Darth Vader Star Wars outfit with his great big sword. "This will frighten them," he reassured himself.

He crept silently around and was careful not to make a sound. Tiptoeing into Lilly's room, he sat on her bed and shook her slightly.

"Lilly, wake up. I think there's someone downstairs," he whispered.

Lilly sat up in her bed. "What time is it?" she said, rubbing her eyes. Satsuma scuttled off the bed.

Frankie pulled down the bedclothes.

"Get dressed. We need to see what's happening."

Lilly fumbled around and found her dressing gown.

"Well if you're wearing your Darth Vader suit, I'm going to put on my octopus outfit" she whispered. So she grabbed her turquoise and yellow rubber octopus, which was lying crumpled at the bottom of her wardrobe. She lifted up the great big rubbery mass and placed it over her head. It had two holes for her eyes. The long tentacles trailed along the ground as she made her way out on to the landing.

"Take that stupid thing off. How can you walk with that?" Frankie said.

"I'll frighten them in this outfit," she said.

"I'm ringing 999," Frankie said, lifting up the phone on the landing and speaking to a voice at the other end.

They crept down and stood at the bottom of the stairs and watched as two hooded men upended the drawers in the dining room. Papers fluttered in mid-air, cushions landed on the floor, and chairs fell over. The men wore masks and rubber gloves and removed paintings from the wall, as well as placing pieces of silver in a great leather bag.

The children were scared watching the men as they ransacked the contents of the room. Lilly could not contain herself any longer and rushed into the room.

"Stop! Put that down – that's my mother's!" she shouted, approaching the man and waving her octopus tentacles furiously at him. The man was upending Patricia's silver casket on the wooden table and turned around. He dropped the casket and shoved Lilly out of the way. Lilly's tentacles wobbled furiously and she briefly lost her balance. Outside the house in the driveway, lights flashed and sirens blared.

Frankie waved his sword at the men and shouted at Lilly.

"Lilly. Get up. Open the door now, and let them in!" Lilly tripped over her tentacles, but still managed to make her way clumsily to the front door.

"Let's get out of here. Quick!" one of the men uttered. At this stage, Patricia walked into the room, as the men smashed a window in the conservatory at the side and tried to escape.

"Children, what on earth is happening?" yelled their mother frantically. Patricia stood still in the doorway in her long white dressing gown. She could not believe what was going on. Lilly opened the front door for the policemen, as the men were climbing out of the conservatory window. One of the policemen with a great bright torch rushed over and grabbed one of them, in a lock, as he tried to escape. The policeman quickly placed the thief in handcuffs. The second man darted around outside in the moonlight and tried to escape through the back of the garden by climbing over the side gate, but the police dog was too fast for him. As the man attempted to scale the gate, the dog caught his trouser leg and yanked him back. He then fell to the ground, coming face to face with a fierce dog which barked and bared his teeth.

Patricia ran up to Frankie and Lilly.

"Oh, children, thank goodness you are both safe. What on earth happened?" she stammered, hugging each child.

"I heard a noise, and I woke Lilly, and I called the police," stammered Frankie, in between long breaths of excitement, as he put his sword back into his sheath. "Oh, what a brave pair you are!" said his mother, stroking his hair.

"Mum, you can't send us away now after what has happened," whimpered Lilly through her octopus outfit.

"Oh, we'll have to rethink about sending you away. What would I do without my two little watch dogs?" Patricia said, trying to hold back the tears.

September arrived, and Frankie and Lilly were afraid that they would soon be sent away.

"Children, I now realise that if you were to go away to school, it would be very lonely here for us. So we have decided not to send you to boarding school, but only if you behave at home. If you don't behave, one of you will go away and the other can stay with me, as together you are quite a handful. Is that clear?"

The children rushed and hugged their mother.

"Oh, Mum, we knew you would never send us away!"

Susannah and the Pearl Rose

Susannah was a little girl who lived in a fine house where her parents kept guests. The house was situated near a well-kept green park not far from the city centre.

Susannah was eight years old. She had two older sisters who were nearly grown up, so apart from Bobo, her Siamese cat, Farrelly the hamster, and Mr MacLafferty, the gardener, she had few friends. She preferred her imaginary friends to any children who lived locally or from her school.

Each day Susannah strolled through the nearby public park with Elena, the Danish au pair girl on her way home from school. Elena was tall with deep golden hair tied up with glittering blue glass combs. In the park among the trees a calm lake nestled, which was home to ducks, squirrels, swans, moorhens, garden birds and, of course, seagulls, who came to snatch the bread that the children gave to the ducks. There was a small island in the centre of the lake, with a small hut made of bamboo and palm tree leaves, where many wild creatures and birds made their home. People loved the hut's quirky shape; it was like a great big tea cosy with a bobble of wild flowers and leaves on its top, which looked like a colourful chimney.

One day Susannah refused to accompany Elena back home, as she wanted to climb onto a leafy sycamore tree with some low-lying branches, but the au pair scolded her.

"You cannot climb this tree. You'll get hurt, and then what'll I say to your mummy? You can't just go scampering off wherever you like. It is a big dangerous city and you have to careful," Elena said harshly.

But Susannah kicked and screamed and sat on the side of the road, refusing to move. "I want to be like other children who can climb trees, get dirty, and have snotty noses and freckles, instead of always having to wear a sun hat, or stay inside when it rains," the little girl grumbled.

"Listen, Susie, if you behave and come along home for your supper, I'll sing you a song. Wouldn't you like that?"

But still the child refused to move. She hid her face in her hands.

"No, I don't want to hear any of your songs."

"And maybe if you're very good, I'll buy you an ice-cream," Elena said.

"I don't want an ice-cream. I want to climb the tree," Susannah bawled. When Elena turned her back to pick up her hat which had blown away, Susannah quickly ran over to the tree and started to climb. She tugged and pulled and heaved herself up on the low-lying branches and soon had climbed half way up.

"Yippee, I'm up in my tree castle and I can see the whole city from here," Susannah squealed with excitement.

Elena was furious.

"Get down at once from that tree, or I'll call the police and what's more I shall tell your parents and they will never let you out again." But Susannah sat on the branch, singing to herself.

The minutes passed and then an hour and finally as people began to stroll home from work, the little girl slowly climbed down from the tree.

Elena caught Susannah before she plopped to the ground.

"You are a very naughty girl. I don't know what I am going to do with you. You really frightened me as you climbed so high," Elena said with tears beginning to form in her eyes. She was so relieved that the little girl was back down safely on the ground.

How Susannah longed for Bobo and Farrelly to respond when she spoke to them. But they remained silent. Bobo lay curled up all day long on her favourite armchair and Farrelly was so busy tunnelling that he had little time for anything else.

"Mum, why can't I have a dog?" the little girl pleaded with her mother one day.

"Dogs are too troublesome in a city." Her mother had heard her child's request for a dog so often before. So Susannah would pretend that Bobo was a dog and would tie a small lead around the cat's neck, but the wary Siamese got as far as the door and raced up the stairs again, terrified of the traffic. The child would then sit at the bottom of the stairs and start to talk to her imaginary friends.

Susannah made up friends to keep her company and

she had many of them. Her favourite imaginary friend was Josephine. Josephine was fearless and daring; she would climb out of the upstairs window, scoot down the drainpipe and skip through the narrow city streets with Susannah. Together they had a wonderful time. They would prance around large grey monuments with frivolous fairies in the dawn, ride on cool swans' backs on the river and fly and dart like swallows from the many church spires seen from Susannah's bedroom window. Oh, how she dreamed of an exciting life with Josephine.

Susannah loved nothing more than to sit in the guest-house dining room at a table in a corner, on which she would lay her dolls' tea set of pale blue speckled china. She would pretend that she and Josephine were having tea together just like grown-ups.

She would pour 'pretend tea' from the teapot, and speak to Josephine across the table. "Well, Josie, my dear, what did you buy today?"

Then, laughing out loud, her voice would become high-pitched and excited, just the way she imagined Josephine would speak. "I've been invited to a ball, but I couldn't possibly wear the gown I wore last year. Lots of important people will be invited, so I must make sure to dress very, very well."

"What'll you wear?" Susannah squealed, her sapphire blue eyes wide with excitement.

Josephine thought for a minute.

"I'll wear a dress of the finest seaweed, with a twinkling tiara on my head made of ivy with precious stones from the sea."

"Wow," Susannah said, placing her tiny hands on the top of her blonde curls.

"And great bright rubies, the size of pigeon eggs, for my necklace," Josephine said, as Susannah made a small circle with her finger and thumb around her soft little neck.

Without taking a breath, Josephine continued. "And I'd have gloves, shiny and golden as the sun, made from the finest sand, which would melt and fall away at dawn." Stretching out her arms, thin as sticks, Josephine showed the imaginary gloves.

"Oh, do please let me see the dress!" Susannah asked her imaginary friend.

Stepping out into the middle of the floor, Susannah pretended to open boxes, throwing aside tissue paper, just like her mother did, and lovingly hold up the make-believe ball-gown.

But Susannah ached and longed for real freedom and fun. So one night, when everybody was asleep, she peeped out of her bedroom window and spied the sky twinkling with stars and the pale moon dipping in and out of small wispy clouds.

"Hi, little stars. Oh, how I'd love to play with you under the moonlight."

They seemed to beckon to her to venture out in the cool night air. As the clock struck midnight, she hatched a plan.

"I'll wait until everybody is in bed, and then I'll slip out through the back door," she murmured excitedly to herself.

So when the great big grandfather clock in the hall chimed three o'clock, Susannah put on her favourite red dress and slipped her tiny feet into pink satin slippers and tiptoed past Elena's room. She crept down the stairs, out past the main reception, where the night porter at the desk was busy on his computer. The little girl let herself out the back door into the refreshing night air, brushed past the bushes in the garden and made her way out on to the street. Apart from the odd car, nothing moved among the eerie shadows.

Susannah carefully tiptoed along the silent street which led to the park, not far from the house. She felt free at last, carefree with the moon and the stars, who smiled down on her as if to say, "Don't be frightened, little one. We'll guide you through the night."

Although the park was closed at night, Susannah had figured out how to squeeze through a narrow opening down by the side of the main gates and let herself in. Fearless, she ambled along by the edge of the lake. Peering into the rippling water, she saw her reflection, as well as strange dappled shapes moving in the water under the moonlight. But she recalled Elena's words of warning: "The lake is deep and dark, so be very careful not to go too close to the edge or you might fall in."

The little girl walked along and then sat down on a large grey stone under a drooping rose. Its leaves were dry and parched and brown in parts. Having pity on it, Susannah got up on her tiptoes and whispered, "Poor rose, you're not as pretty as Mr MacLafferty's roses in our garden at home."

Then she leaned over, peered into one of its limp heads and kissed it.

Wrapping her tiny arms around the poor sad rose and hugging its drooping head, she sang a lullaby Elena had taught her.

Then she said, "Don't worry, little one. Someday you'll be lovely too."

The tired little girl sat back down on the cold hard stone and drifted off to sleep. The moon and stars crept back into their night caves to make way for the slender light of the dawn.

When the mighty sun crept up into the morning sky, Susannah awoke suddenly on the grey marble stone in the park. She could hear the birds twittering in the trees overhead. Tired and shivering, she stretched herself and yawned.

"I best be getting back to my bed before Mummy finds out that I'm gone. Goodbye rose," she said as she blew the rose a kiss. She headed off and skipped down the pathway, out of the park in the direction of home. The man at reception in the guesthouse was snoring quietly and Susannah tiptoed past him, crept up the stairs and fell into her soft bed.

Meanwhile back in the park Susannah's songs and gentle words had breathed life back into the faded white rose she had left behind. Within several hours, its small rose head burst into large beautiful snow-white petals, filling the air with the sweet scent of honey.

Some days later Susannah and Elena were walking through the park. The child ran to the edge of the lake and stopped at the large stone where she had seen the dull lifeless rose that night. She gasped in amazement at what she saw. The rose had completely transformed into a magnificent flower. Bumble bees hovered around the rose in their eager attempt to crawl inside its smoothly cupped rose petals and bask in its fragrance. Susannah was very excited.

She ran and put her arms around the magnificent fragrant rose. The most exquisite perfume came from its beautiful petals. Gone was the straggly, withered stem. Instead shiny leaves grew on a strong stem with big healthy red thorns. The rose had a great head of pearl coloured petals curling at the edges, as it stood tall and erect. It dazzled the air with its beauty.

"Oh, rose, you're much too grand for a vase! You'll never be thrown away on the scrap heap. I hope that you'll bloom and bloom the whole summer through," Susannah cried gleefully. The beautiful rose swayed its proud head in the soft sunny breeze as if it understood these words from the little girl.

An old lady passed by and whispered to Elena, "Beautiful rose, isn't it? I've never seen anything like it, and I've been coming here for years."

Elena looked at her and then at centre of the rose. But the old lady continued, "It's a real beauty. No one seems to know what it's called, not even the park attendant. He says he's never seen anything quite as magnificent."

Elena wondered about the lovely flower in front of her. Susannah looked up at Elena and the au pair took the child's hand and looked into her sparkling blue eyes and said, "It's a beautiful rose, isn't it? What'll we call it?"

The little girl thought for a minute. "Oh, I know!" she gasped. "Why don't we call it the 'pearl rose'? It's white like snow and shiny and smooth just like Mummy's pearls."

"So that will be the beautiful rose's name and it will be our little secret," Elena said, hugging Susannah close to her.

Elena and Susannah visited the park most days. Autumn came and the other roses in the park faded and died, their soft petals falling onto the soil beneath, leaving bare stems and rose hips. But the majestic pearl rose bloomed afresh and continued to do so with wondrous petals. The park gardener passed by, admired its cream-tipped petals and moved on with his tools for pruning the other roses. He dared not touch the wonderful rose.

Winter arrived, covering the city with a soft white blanket of snow, and yet the white rose still flowered. The swans glided gracefully on the calm lake water, and when they stopped still, they looked like white marble statues. The fluffy little birds tried to stay warm by ruffling up their feathers, picking berries from the trees or eating crumbs scattered on the ground by passers-by.

But the winter brought colds and flus, and Susannah became ill and had to go to hospital. Outside her room on a terrace, there were bushes planted in pots in memory of all the children who had once been sick there. Susannah's mother and Elena remained at the child's bedside. The doctor felt the little girl's soft hand and brow for any change in her condition and examined her chest with a stethoscope. He then looked through the chart at her bedside. His brow was furrowed and he seemed rather worried. He looked gravely at the two ladies and said in a low whisper, "We shall need to wait and see how your child responds to the medication. Hopefully we should see a change in her condition in the next day or so. Have courage and faith."

Her mother sobbed as she clutched her child's hand and laid her cheek against the child's fingers. "My poor little Susie, please, please get better, darling," she whimpered into her handkerchief.

Elena wrung out a soft cloth under a cold tap and placed it on the child's hot forehead to soothe her. "Susannah, darling, please stay with us, please, please," she said silently to herself as she cried.

Susannah clutched her long green toy caterpillar as she dipped in and out of the fever which was raging inside her weak body. Her father paced the floor nervously. "We should never have let her out in the wind and rain that afternoon. I told you she would catch cold," he said curtly looking at the two ladies sitting at the bedside. A fan hummed and whirred cool air in the child's sickroom.

Susannah was so weak that she was barely able to take a breath, and her mother feared the worst. "Oh, my darling, please don't go! Hold my hand," she said sobbing into her crumpled tissue.

Elena leaned over the bed and mopped her wet brow. "Darling you must get better, because Bobo and Farrelly are wondering where you are. You see the house is very quiet without you. Poor Mr MacLafferty is very sad all the time."

One night, when all was still, Susannah awoke from a disturbing dream and heard the sound of something rustling at the window pane. Her mother had drifted off to sleep at her bedside, as she had had no sleep for several nights. Elena had gone home. Outside, the howling, raging winds had died down and soft snow tumbled onto the ground beneath.

The little girl threw off the hot damp sheets from her bed and tottered to the large bay window looking out onto the terrace. Susannah rubbed the frosted pane and peered outside. Turning the key in the door, she looked wondrously out at the snow-filled scene. Oh, it was good to feel the fresh cool night breeze on her face again!

"Hello, snowflakes. You're like tiny ballerinas," the child gasped as she watched in amazement as they tumbled and twirled around her. She held out her hand to catch a falling flake, but it just melted in her fingers.

All of a sudden, she felt something drop at her feet. She looked down and saw that it was a single white rose. Bend-

ing down, she picked up the limp, once beautiful flower. She smelled the sweetest scent from the rose. Although wet and slightly withered, the rose had never lost its magnificent perfume. Pressing its drooping petals to her lips, she remembered the night in the park.

"Hello, pearl rose," she murmured. As the child held the rose to her, its fragile petals fell to the ground one by one, scattering in the cold night air. A thorn pricked her finger. Some drops of blood fell onto the snow below. Susannah bent down and stuck the rose into a large pot filled with snow-covered earth where her drops of blood had fallen. She blew a kiss at it.

"I hope you will be a beautiful flower next year. Goodbye, pearl rose." The child then felt weak from the cold night air and fell against the door. Her mother awoke in alarm and rushed over to Susannah, who collapsed into her arms.

"Nurse, quick, Susannah has collapsed. Come quickly," the mother screamed. They brought the little girl inside from the cold and placed on the bed. There she soon drifted into a deep sleep.

The next morning Susannah lay sleeping peacefully. Her breathing was calm and untroubled, and the fever which had gripped her frail body seemed to have left her. Her cheeks, once pale, had now a faint rosy colour. Everything was still but for the hushed sound of falling snow. The tiny birds tried to keep their bodies warm as the sun shone through the pale clouds.

When the doctor called, he was surprised at the change in the sick child. He looked at his watch as he felt her pulse and put his hand on her brow. He turned to her mother and said, "Your little girl is going to get better. She is strong and a great little fighter. The worst seems to have passed."

Susannah's mother moved her eyes from her sick child to the doctor and said tearfully, "That is wonderful news. But I must tell you something strange and wonderful that happened during the night. I can't remember too much, except that I seemed to have fallen into a deep sleep. I have not been sleeping and was very tired last night. Then I was woken by a noise, and I got up to find my little darling on the balcony, drenched with melted snow." She dabbed a tear from her eye, glancing at the sleeping child, and added, "It's as if a miracle happened...so very strange."

Each day brought an improvement in the child's condition. From her bedroom window Susannah watched her pearl rose take root in the cold ground outside. After a week she left the hospital and returned home. All the while the pearl rose got stronger in the soil.

The following summer a beautiful white rose blossomed in the large flower pot where the drops of blood had fallen from Susannah's finger and where she had planted the rose. The exquisite white rose bloomed the whole season through, and everybody in the hospital marvelled at its beauty and fragrance. They also wondered how it had got there.

This whole experience of Susannah's illness prompted her parents to sell their guesthouse and move to the country, where their child could enjoy life away from the buzz and noise of the inner city.

"Darling, we are going to move down the country.

Wouldn't you love that?" "Oh, Mummy, could I have hens, bunnies, pigeons and maybe a pony?" Susannah asked eagerly.

"Darling, you can have anything you want, even a pony. You would be busy looking after them and as you know animals need lots of love and care and well, they could be your companions too," her mother said, pressing the child gently to her.

So the family moved away from the city to a place where Susannah ran among the meadows and cycled everywhere. Elena accompanied Susannah and they continued to be the best of friends.

When Susannah was a little older her parents bought her a lively pony, whom she named Snowball. Snowball and Susannah were rarely apart.

The rose no longer bloomed in the park, as its spirit and loveliness were now blooming in the children's hospital garden. But only Susannah knew how the pearl rose had brought her back to health and was now flowering in the hospital garden where she had left it. Susannah was healed by its strength and presence on that great wintry stormy night. This secret she would always carry in her heart.

The Sugar Peach Tree

"Whirr, whirr, whirr…" sounded her wings as Betty Butterfly flew from flower to flower. The garden creatures loved to see her flutter around, as she was friendly, chatting to all about everything that was happening in the garden and beyond. The flowers could not move, so they relied on Betty for all the gossip and news. She was a beautiful creature: her elegant white wings each had two black spots

and their edges were piped with grey and blue. Her body had two delicate feelers which she used to probe into the centre of the flowers.

In the garden lived many other creatures. There was little Ladybird, known as Lady, with her perfect shell of orange and tiny black spots. She especially liked the white rose, as it had a heavenly smell and there was always the lure of a nice fat juicy greenfly. Another resident in the garden was Snail, known as Solo, as he tended to keep to himself a lot. Solo was slow and a bit grumpy because he had to carry a huge brown shell on his back and took a long time to travel anywhere. He could never hide; everybody knew where to find him, since he left a silver trail of slime everywhere he went. Finally there was Connie the spider. Connie was always busy and rarely had any time for gossip or listening to the woes of others. She spent her days laying eggs, trapping dragonflies and weaving her wondrous webs in various places in the garden shed. The creatures knew not to dare venture into any of Connie's strange and complicated webs.

These tiny creatures lived in a fine big garden belonging to an old lady. It was pretty with flowers of many colours: lilac, lemon and crimson. All summer long, Sun's laughing face in the turquoise sky watched over all this close-knit little family in the garden.

One day things changed dramatically for the creatures. Betty fluttered around with the latest piece of news.

"I have heard from some busy bees that workmen are to come with giant machines to knock down the old lady's house and garden in order to widen the road," she gasped.

"Help! Help! I'm going to be cut down!" cried a poor helpless yellow flower with tears in her eyes. Betty and Lady tried to console her, but she was distraught.

As the four friends, Betty, Lady, Solo and Connie, sat on a holly tree watching and waiting, they wondered what would happen to them. For once Solo saw the advantage of having his own house.

"At least I have my shell," he mumbled and went back into hiding, fearful of these men with their machines and diggers.

"We can't go to the house next door, as its garden has no flowers or bushes, only a long dull lawn," murmured Lady.

"The house on the other side has that big marmalade cat called Pudsey, who loves to chase butterflies," sighed Betty.

Connie had more news.

"I have been busy spinning my webs and heard from some friendly bees that the old lady is moving away and she has hired a small van to remove all of her plants to another garden, far away from here," but like all clever spiders, she had a great plan.

"I've got a super idea. Why don't we all go to this wonderful garden too?" she said wondering if any of the holly branches would be suitable to spin a web.

"But how?" asked Solo, who never ventured too far and who was always a bit wary of anyone who was adventurous.

"Well, we can climb onto some plants and be taken there," the smart spider said swinging from a piece of a thread she had just woven. Connie always came up with good ideas, as she knew how to set up her web anywhere, be it on a ceiling or in a corner or even on the mirror of a car.

"Well, I think that's a wonderful idea, but we must be careful to hide among the plants so that we can arrive safely. While I simply love my black and orange back, it is instantly noticeable," Lady said flapping her wings.

So when a red van arrived and the plants were being loaded on to it, the little creatures got ready to climb inside. Solo was a bit slow at first, but he finally managed to haul himself up and settled on a broad comfortable shiny leaf. Betty fixed herself on the same plant so that she could keep an eye on him in case he fell off. Little Lady nestled on a carpet of pollen on a bright yellow orchid flower, while Connie lay on a large fern and hoped that they would arrive sooner rather than later.

Off they sped with the rare plants in the red van across the country.

"Oh, I feel a bit dizzy, and I can't say that I like this horrible smell. It's a bit like the smell from that awful lawn mower," moaned Solo.

"Now, now, never mind, you just settle down to have a nice munch of these small weeds growing in this flower pot," Lady said stroking his slimy back with a fluttering wing.

They finally arrived at the coast. They all climbed over to the small window in the van and strained to look out.

"Oh, look, I can see white-tipped waves and children playing on the beach making sandcastles," said Betty enthusiastically, and she began to flap her wings with excitement.

"We're here at last," called Connie as she thrust herself up to the pane of glass and peered out of the misty window.

"Oh, I'm really looking forward to landing on a nice cool sweet-smelling rose," sighed Lady, who was feeling just a little bit hot at this stage.

"I'd love a bit of a nice juicy lettuce leaf," chuckled Solo, who had an enormous appetite.

There it lay before them, Ballinclea House, and its wonderful garden. There were tall shrubs in every colour

and massive bunches of flowers waving in the soft summer breeze, as if to welcome the new arrivals. Tiny bunches of flowers grew at the foot of trees like clusters of precious stones. Everything seemed to be bursting with colour and life. Over by the wood, a pond was covered with giant pink water lilies, where proud swans glided with their snow-white feathers puffed out proudly on their backs.

But there in the middle of the lawn stood quite the most beautiful tree they had ever seen. Its wide branches covered the entire lawn like a gigantic umbrella from which hung golden peaches twinkling in the sun.

"Goodbye, friendly plants, and thank you so much for allowing us to hide in your precious leaves," the four said as they left the van and made their way across the lawn to the shady woods. Soon they were greeted by some friendly bees.

"Welcome, welcome," the bees all buzzed together. "There is plenty of room for you all here, lots of flowers, water, and food – as much as you like, but the only thing which is forbidden is that peach tree over there. It grows fruit all year round. However, no one eats the fruit or even touches its leaves or blossoms," hummed a large bumblebee. He was barely able to move, he was so full of nectar.

The newly arrived creatures wondered at this piece of news. "Why? What would happen if we ate from the peach tree?" asked Solo, who was always partial to a nice bite of a juicy fruit. The bees were silent. Then one bee dropped onto the ground near them.

"You would fall into a deep sleep, never to waken," he said as he sidled off to the hive.

They all fell silent against as they settled down, each finding a little patch of garden to make their home, but nobody ventured near the peach tree.

A little girl called Julia lived in Ballinclea House and

spent many an afternoon in the garden. All of the insects and creatures that lived in the garden loved Julia, as she was very gentle and kind to all of them. She would take them up tenderly in her tiny hand and let them down delicately on a beautiful rose or dewy leaf.

Julia would sing to them and tell them little stories, and when they were not feeling well her soft touch would always restore their good health again.

Betty loved to perch on Julia's soft golden hair when the child slept or read her book, or played on her swing in the garden. Betty would imagine that she was in a great big valley as she meandered in and out of the parting in the centre of the child's head and among her tresses. She would then climb and explore inside the great big yellow ribbon

which gathered up the hair at the back of Julia's neck, and get lost in its folds and knots and fall asleep.

"Pretty butterfly, what lovely wings you have! I wish that I had wings like yours, and I'd fly, fly away," murmured Julia, stroking the little butterfly's wings gently and blowing her soft child's breath on to the insect's delicate wings. Betty trusted Julia and spent her afternoons sleeping among the child's soft curls when she had got tired of flying from flower to flower.

Connie busied herself with setting up a web under a young blackbird's nest in a nearby honeysuckle tree. She hummed ancient spider songs to herself, songs that had been handed down to her through generations of spiders as they wove their webs. The nest was a neat cup-shaped

one, lined with mud. The spider climbed to the edge of the nest and peered in with her sharp little eyes. She saw four blue-green eggs covered with red-brown speckles. She was anxious to throw out her silk from her position in the nest to the nearest branch, but then the nervous blackbird spied her and set up a ferocious din, screeching and hopping around the poor frightened spider.

"Get out of my nest, you horrible creature, before I eat you. You'll have the entire bush covered in dead insects in your horrible web, and my babies will soon be hatched and learning to fly." The blackbird created such a shrieking sound that poor Connie scuttled for her life with all her eight legs down the tree and along the grass. She rested under a pink camellia whose flowers were beginning to fade and fall.

"Well, I won't go near her nest again. What a fussy bird!" Connie said as she fell asleep and dreamt a spider's dream of flies and dragonflies and silver webs in faraway lands ruled solely by spiders.

One hot summer's day Solo was resting under the shade of some long ferns and Lady was snoozing inside a perfumed white rose petal. Julia moved her chair under the peach tree to be in its shade out of the sun.

Betty dozed on Julia's soft hair. A light breeze blew and a drop of peach juice fell on to the child's forehead. Julia dropped the book that she was reading and fell into a deep sleep. Betty fluttered around the child to keep her cool. But Julia did not wake up. There was pandemonium in the house when Julia could not be awakened.

"Julia, darling, time to get up," her mother frantically cried, holding her only child, but Julia lay lifeless in her arms. Her mother took her inside and called the doctor. Her parents sought help and advice from far and wide, but to no avail. Julia remained in a deep sleep.

The little creatures of the garden were full of grief, as Julia was one of their dearest friends. The house was in mourning. Everyone went around with a sad expression on their faces. Despair and grief descended on the place.

Wind heard about the sad fate of the little girl from a young thrush that was heading to the great icy northern shores. He immediately changed into a strong tailwind and headed back to the garden of Ballinclea. Wind, who was very wise and knew almost everything, having whirled all

over the world, looked gravely at the small creatures in the garden, puffed himself up and said in a deep voice,

"Legend has it that once a powerful king lived here in Ballinclea House. One summer's day his only son, while playing in the garden, fell from this beautiful tree and tragically died," he said, blowing a great big puff in the direction of the peach tree. The king wept for a long time, and was so enraged that he cast a spell over this magnificent fruit tree. From then on, its leaves and fruit would cause a deep sleep in those who tasted of its fruit juice.

"We'll chop it down!" the villagers cried. But the sad king forbade them.

"If any of you attempt to cut down this wretched tree, I shall have them banished forever from my kingdom. I want to leave it to remind me of my son who died."

And so it was that the tree grew into the magnificent tree that you see before you today," puffed Wind.

"But how can we break the spell?" asked an eager bee.

"That is a good question. The spell can only be broken by planting a peach stone from the only remaining tree of its kind, which grows in a land far, far away from here."

"And where is this land?" questioned Lady.

"The Land of the Sugar Peach Tree," puffed the wise Wind.

The little creatures listened in silence as old Wind spoke to them about his plans to save Julia from her great sleep. Howling and whooshing, he continued, "I shall set off to this far away land and return with a stone from the sugar peach tree to be planted in this garden."

167

But Connie was inquisitive.

"I don't understand. How will the stone help?" she said, scuttling on to another branch.

Wind replied, "Here it will grow and flower, and at the first flowering, the king's wicked spell will be broken. Then, and only then, will the child come back to life. I shall head off south immediately to the Land of the Sugar Peach Tree. But I shall need somebody who can identify which peach will be the one to save our little girl. You see, while I am big and strong, I know little about fruits and flowers."

"Please, please, Wind, may I accompany you? You see, I can find the finest of fruits and the most colourful flowers," piped up Betty.

"Wind, Wind, I would like to come with you too. I can parachute myself on a blade of grass which you can take up in a gust. I could keep Betty company," the spider said, looking around the little group.

"Oh, yes, Connie, that would be just wonderful. I can see the two of us flying together on a great adventurous journey, across miles and miles of seas and mountains. Please, please Wind, can Connie come too?" Betty asked as she fluttered her little wings with excitement.

"Oh, that would be marvellous. It would be a great adventure," said Connie, as she headed off to make plans for this massive journey ahead of them.

"So our peach tree carries a dark and tragic secret," Lady murmured.

"Precisely," confirmed Wind. Although Betty and Connie were frightened, they had great confidence in Wind.

Wind was ready to head south.

"We must not delay," he roared.

Lady flew to wish him goodbye. She gave him a flower necklace, which she had made with some of the other insects, and Solo rubbed some special snail slime on to Wind's breath to give him strength. Connie wove a web of the finest silk and threw it in Wind's direction.

"My web will keep you strong and remind you of your task," she said, and waddled off on her eight legs to seek out a fresh blade of grass and release a line of silk to await the gust of wind which would whisk her up like a parachute.

"Goodbye, my little friends!" Wind whirled and puffed and was gone. As he roared, he gathered up Connie and Betty in his great breath.

"Goodbye, Wind! God speed and good luck!" the garden creatures all chanted.

He soared up into the sky, puffing higher and higher into the clouds until he disappeared, roaring and howling. Some friendly seagulls kept him company until they spied a fishing boat offloading some fish into the sea and swerved away from him. On and on he blew and bellowed. The sea was no longer the bright blue of the day, but now a dismal grey. He met Rain, and they chatted for a while until she headed off to meet some angry grey clouds over on the horizon.

"Goodbye, Wind. Good luck with your quest," Rain rattled her long grey wet skirt made of droplets and pelted off out to the horizon.

On and on Wind puffed in his quest to find the sugar

peach stone for Julia and the little creatures of the garden. Sun came out beaming with content.

"Hi there, Wind. You seem to be in a hurry. Why don't you take it easy and enjoy some of my lovely sunbeams?"

But Wind had no time to delay with the gleeful Sun, who loved to laugh and joke. He was, after all, on a very secret and important mission. Connie and Betty kept each other company on the journey south with Wind.

"Lucky you, having your blade of grass, which you can use as a parachute. I have only my poor fragile wings, and so I feel very tired," cried Betty when they were way up among the cold great clouds.

"Now, don't give up. Have courage, Betty. Soon we shall be in the Land of the Sugar Peach Tree, when the sun will shine all day," whispered Connie.

Betty thought that Connie was such a clever creature, being able to make these very complicated webs that she trusted the spider and was reassured with these kind spider words.

When Wind, Connie and Betty had departed for the Land of the Sugar Peach Tree, all of the little creatures of the garden at Ballinclea House became sad and forlorn. They remained silent and rarely ventured out from under their hideaways. Solo stayed under a large green bush with lots of flowers and Lady tucked herself away inside her favourite pearly white rose bloom.

The gardener came with a giant suction machine, hoovering up all the brown crinkly-shaped leaves and tossing them all around. Lady and Solo were sucked up in the great machine and ended up in the garden shed, where the door banged behind them. Before they could get out, the door was suddenly bolted shut by the gardener. It was very cold and dark inside the shed. As they looked around they could see lots of garden tools, a lawn mower, and sacks of seeds and tins of all kinds containing oil, glue and paint. Solo felt very sick.

"Oh, the smell of petrol is making me ill. I need a nice rich juicy lettuce leaf to settle my tummy."

Lady felt sorry for him. He was such a grumpy old fellow and could not really put up with much. She was going to have to think of a way out.

"Oh, I declare, Autumn can't be trusted. He just blows everything up and about in the air. Now we must stay calm and think of a plan." They both then settled down in a corner of the shed under a sack and waited and watched and schemed of ways to escape.

Days passed, but nobody came to open the door. Solo became very upset. He hated this dry place, preferring nice damp ones with lots of old rotting plants. Also, he had to get ready for hibernation and eat plenty, and there was nothing to eat here. Lady dreamed of all the juicy aphids she was missing on her favourite rose tree. But luck was at hand.

Soon they heard murmurings outside the garden shed, and suddenly the bolt shot back and in came the gardener, in his big rubber boots. He started to rummage through the various sacks, humming to himself.

"Now's our chance. We really must be ready to move

out that door, before it's snapped shut again," Lady said hurriedly to herself. She knew that this was their only chance to escape. So, mustering all her strength, she awakened Solo, who poked his head out from under his shell. He looked very tired and sleepy.

"Look, wake up. Now, I know that you're very weak, but this is our last chance to escape. The door is open. Quick, get your snail foot to move, and once we're over the threshold we are out and away from this horrid old garden shed," Lady said trying to get him to move by dancing and whirring over his shell. "Oh, my poor shell seems so very heavy all of a sudden," the snail sighed. But Lady guided him slowly out across the cold concrete floor until she could see the dark grey clouds outside and hear the birds singing.

"Oh, look at the lovely grass outside with lots of juicy morsels; come on, just a little more to go," Lady said. Solo was very slow. He seemed to take forever to move. They both tottered out gently until finally they crossed the threshold and were out and away from that dreary old shed. Lady breathed a sigh of relief.

"Oh, isn't it lovely to be out in the fresh air again, to smell the freshness of everything. Now we must ensure that you get settled in a nice shady place with a big juicy plant to munch." Solo found a place to rest and immediately tucked into some nice moist rotting compost. He chomped on a huge bite of wet newly mown hay and had another bite and then another. He then promptly fell fast asleep, exhausted but relieved, and dreamt a snail's dream that he was being fanned down by strange-looking black beetles waving giant lettuce leaves in a large rainforest far away.

Meanwhile, Lady flew off up to her favourite white rose bush to feast on some fat greenfly. When she had gorged herself sufficiently, she crept inside a soft wet rose and fell asleep.

After a long time of battling his way south, Wind finally arrived at the Land of the Sugar Peach Tree. It lay out to the west and was separated from the mainland by water during a full tide. As the sea levels fell, leaving only sand, many people thought that they could reach the land by walking across the sand to this magic island. But the island always disappeared into the mists, and they could never reach it.

No person lived there. It was a place where only plants, insects and small animals dwelt.

"Oh, we're here at last!" screamed Connie as she swung and whirled on her parachute.

"Oh, look out there, see the island!" Betty said. She was always interested in new places and flowers on which to alight.

"The air smells of peaches and roses. It is more beautiful than I had ever imagined," Connie said, stretching herself up on her parachute.

"Can you hear the sounds of whispering streams? Listen. And what great big beautiful roses of every colour with large soft petals – just where I want to lie down and rest my poor tired wings," sighed Betty. She could sleep and sleep, she was so exhausted after her long journey that had taken them across seas and mountains in all weather. The flowers shook their crisp leaves and nodded their proud beautiful crowns at the travellers. But Wind was on a secret mission and hurriedly passed them by. He could not delay as he had to bring back the precious stone to awaken the little girl.

The beauty of the island dazzled Wind. Being the northern wind, he was used to the bleak Arctic wastes, but he knew that he must continue on his journey. He flew around the place searching for the Sugar Peach trees, but could find none.

On and on he puffed and blew, but he could not find where the trees grew. He was almost giving up when Betty spied the most wonderful sight she had ever beheld.

"There, over the horizon, look, look, can you see a whole orchard of sugar peach trees glistening in the noonday sun? My, what a sight!" Betty was excited.

Wind hurled on and approached the orchard. There were hundreds of wonderful fruit trees. Their fruits were soft, ripe and ready to fall. Each tree drooped down with the weight of its full golden peaches, dripping with juice. Each peach sparkled with crisp golden sugar glaze, twinkling in the sunshine. The sight took Wind's breath away. He knew that he had to bring back a stone from one of these precious fruits, so, venturing over, he hovered around some of the trees.

"Oh dear, now where shall we start?" He could not make up his mind.

"Which is the one true tree with the precious stone which would save Julia?" Connie wondered.

"There are rows and rows of trees, each tree more beautiful than the next, but I can hop from tree to tree and pick out the tree with the most delicious fruit" observed Betty.

"Why that's a great idea Betty," whooshed Wind. Then along strutted a cheeky yellow-crested white cockatoo.

"Oh, hello, Mr Cockatoo, you are looking lovely today. You must be very proud of your handsome feathers," Connie said.

The vain bird strutted and puffed out his sleek white feathers, etched with crimson and gold, and nodded his

bright crest. He was the envy of all the other birds on the island.

"Why, thank you, spider. You are most kind," said

the bird, who was always partial to a bit of flattery.

Having softened up the bird, Wind decided that the only way to find out anything was to ask the locals.

"I wonder if you can help us please," Wind asked politely.

"Well, that depends on what you want to know," squawked the bird, cocking his head. "I'm looking for the stone of the sugar peach tree which can save a little girl who has fallen into a deep sleep," puffed Wind.

"Ah! You have come to the right place, my friend." But, eager to look out for himself, the cockatoo ventured to ask, "I would like you to do something for me."

Wind wondered what the bird had in mind. "Yes, of course, I'd be happy to help in any way I can. Pray tell me what it is you wish for."

The bird eyed him up with his beady black eyes and puffing his chest out and raising his plumed head said, "I'll show you which tree will give you your precious stone, on one condition; if you take me with you some of the way, back to the forests from where I came. You see, while this island is paradise, I am lonely here. I need tall dark trees of the jungle."

"Why, I'd be happy to," Wind puffed, anxious to get on with the task at hand.

The bird then flew over to a small but perfect tree and, tilting his shiny plumed head, squawked, "I know each tree in this orchard very well and have eaten all of the fruits, but the most perfect and delicious fruits will be found on this beautiful tree here," he said alighting on one of its branches.

"Oh, thank goodness we have found the tree," sighed Betty.

"What luck meeting that saucy bird," exclaimed Connie.

"We'd never have found the one true tree out of this vast orchard without your help," puffed Wind gratefully, nodding to the cockatoo.

"Here is the legendary peach tree whose fruit contains the precious stone you seek," the bird chirped, proud of being the herald of great news. "But alas I don't know which peach to pick," he said letting out a great big sigh.

"Oh, I can do that. I can tell with a flutter of my wings and my antennae which of these beautiful peaches is the one with the precious stone to save Julia's life," said Betty lifting her head and carefully opening and closing her wings in the heat.

Betty flew around among the peaches, whirring and sniffing each one, until at last she stopped and rested on one.

"This is it. I have found the perfect peach. Its perfume is amazing and it is ripe and succulent," she said her voice strong and firm. Betty hovered over the peach, and the bird flew down and plucked it from the tree.

"Well done, Betty. I am so proud of you," Connie said, giving Betty a hug with all her legs.

"But pray tell me, how do we extract the stone from the fruit?" enquired Wind.

"Watch this," said the bird as he gently took the peach in his strong grey claws and eased off the fruity part with his curved beak. There inside lay a perfect peach stone.

"What a clever bird!" chimed Betty.

"Oh, I don't know. That's what birds do. I think he's vain and proud. Remember, it was you, Betty, who was able to pick out the peach from all the other peaches on this magnificent tree," said Connie.

"Now there you are..." the cockatoo held the precious stone up to Wind.

"Why thank you," Wind muttered. Then sensing a change in atmospheric pressure, Wind puffed himself up.

"Now we must get ready to leave before the weather changes and some other wild raging cyclones come along," Wind huffed.

Shortly before sunset Wind lifted the cockatoo up in his strong hot breath, while the bird clasped the precious stone firmly to its beautiful feathery chest.

"Now, Betty and Connie, get ready to head back. We are setting off again, so make sure that you are ready for the big journey home," puffed Wind.

Betty spread her wings and said goodbye to the peach tree, where she had rested. "Thank you, peach tree, for your beautiful scent. I shall always remember how happy I was here. I feel so well and rested now and ready for the journey back home," she sighed as she kissed the magnificent peach tree goodbye.

Connie moved among the soft lawn, selected a blade of grass, and got herself into position. She sat on a grass seed head, cast out a strand of silk and waited for Wind to whisk her away. "Up, up and away," she chirped. Soon she was riding the gusts of wind and swinging on her grass parachute.

They headed off once more, back north, with some strong southern winds to guide them over the sea on the long journey. Sometime later, they came to the vast green forest in the tropics and here it was time for the bright cockatoo to say goodbye.

"But before I depart, I must meet up with some friendly swallows to pass on the stone," the wise and trustworthy bird said.

A lone swallow passed them and then another and finally some more. The cockatoo watched and selected a strong swallow flying well and keeping good altitude.

Ah yes, the precious stone will be safe with him, thought the clever cockatoo, stopping one in flight. "Hello, swallow. Are you heading north?" the cockatoo asked, flying alongside the swallow.

"Yes, but I can't delay. I must keep going. Sorry, but we must not waste time," the swallow was darting back and forth in the strong wind and was clearly focused on the journey at hand.

"Don't fret, dear swallow. Wind will help you on your great journey north," the cockatoo said to the flying swallow. "But may I ask one favour of you?"

"What is that?" the swallow asked, as he slowed down his flight.

"Please, please take this stone with you to help a little girl," the bird pleaded to the young swallow. "The wind will guide you all the way to her."

"I promise that I shall keep the stone safe," the swallow chirped. He was a young swallow and this was his first great journey north. He reckoned that if he brought the stone safely home that Wind would take care of him and guide him through storms and wild weather.

Wind had the help of some strong winds from southern seas to guide him. When he flew over the large tropical rain forest he descended a little and the eager cockatoo flew off up into a hot air current and landed on one of the tall tropical trees.

"Goodbye, cockatoo, and thank you for all your help in finding the treasured stone. I wish you good luck and hope that you find happiness," called Wind.

"Goodbye, Wind, and safe journey," the cockatoo called out.

Being an inquisitive little butterfly, Betty was anxious to see as much of the world in flight as she could.

"Please, little swallow. Could I beg a ride from you? I'd love to view the world from your fine feathery back. Could I climb on your back at least some of the way?"

"Of course you can, little butterfly," the swallow said

as he buffeted the strong winds and followed the other birds. Betty fluttered up and landed on the gentle swallow's soft shiny back.

"You'd better hold on for dear life as those swallows weave and dart in the air," Connie shouted at her.

"Don't worry. We butterflies are excellent navigators. And so here we go, up and away. Oh, I feel better already," Betty shouted gleefully as she zoomed up in the air on the back of the brave young swallow, which carried the precious peach stone in its beak.

"You're such a clever bird," Betty said later on, as she hung on to him. She noticed that he did everything mid-flight without stopping: cleaning and feeding himself, as well as chatting to some other swallows. Betty noticed that he had a thing which looked like a mini-aeroplane on his back.

"What is that thing on your back, swallow?" Betty asked.

"Oh that. I believe it's called a geolocator."

"A what?" Betty asked, doing another somersault.

"It's to see how far I travel and where I go. Humans put it there to find out more about swallows and our migrations."

Betty had such fun swinging and hanging out from this aeroplane-like attachment. It acted like a trapeze for her. She called to Connie several times, while doing her acrobatics mid-air. "Hi, Connie, watch! Look what I can do!" she screamed excitedly, while swinging on the bar and performing a double somersault. Connie was aghast at the way Betty would turn and weave and spin over and over the swallow's attachment.

At one stage, with a heavy wind, Connie thought that Betty was going to fall off and be lost forever over an ocean. She held her breath.

"Betty, do please be careful. If you fall or miss your balance I won't be able to save you, and the courageous swallow will have to continue on and follow the flock," Connie pleaded with the ever-energetic little butterfly. But brave little Betty swung and dived and pirouetted in mid-air with not a care in the world.

"Oh, don't worry, Connie, we butterflies, although delicate-looking, are hardy and tough little creatures. I'll be just fine. Don't you worry about me!" Betty called gleefully as she did a backflip and landed successfully on the bar perched on the swallow's back.

Wind pushed and dragged himself up and up into the atmosphere and away on his long journey with the swallows. He continued on, puffing and howling, all the time carrying the brave young swallow that in turn carried the wondrous sugar peach stone in its mouth for hundreds of miles across great mountainous peaks and wild seas. Farther north he met a noisy storm, shrieking and spitting, but guided the swallow on until they were both safely back in the garden of Ballinclea House.

When Wind roared in with the swallow, Betty and Connie, the small creatures all rushed out to greet them. They waited, spellbound at the tale of his great journey in quest of the desired stone. The creatures of the garden wondered in awe at the bravery and stamina of this tiny bird that stood in front of them. They all cheered loudly as Wind puffed and huffed.

"It was a long journey, but we made it, thanks to a smart cockatoo who guided us to the right tree and then to Betty who selected the peach. I would also like to thank our brave little swallow here who flew through the storms and bad weather to bring us here." All the creatures clapped and chirped, but the swallow was shy and anxious to get going on his way.

Lady and Solo were thrilled to have Connie and Betty back. Poor Betty was exhausted and her wings were tired and limp.

"We missed you both so much. Life was so dull here in Ballinclea without you two and, of course, Julia. Oh, thank goodness you both made it," chirped Lady.

"It's so good to be back home with all these familiar flowers and our dear friends," Betty said, and they all hugged each other. She then turned to the young swallow and said, "Oh, thank you, little swallow. I couldn't have made the journey back home if it wasn't for you." And she gave him a poke of her antennae.

"I'm glad you made it, beautiful butterfly."

"Goodbye, little swallow, and thank you for keeping me company and carrying me back home safely," Betty said as she flapped her wings at him to say goodbye.

"And now we must plant this precious stone, but firstly we must say goodbye to this wonderful and brave swallow," Wind said with a great puff and huff. The swallow waved to the group and flew off on his journey north.

The creatures received help from the ants, a mole and some friendly squirrels, and set about planting the stone carefully in the sacred earth. Rain offered assistance by

providing some soft showers full of goodness to sprinkle on the ground. Wind had a word with Winter about the treasured sugar peach stone, and Winter promised not to be too harsh with his frost so that the stone could bloom in the soft welcoming earth.

All through the long winter months, Julia lay in a deep sleep. Her distraught mother looked on helplessly as she sat at her child's bedside, wondering what the future held for her precious only little girl.

"Oh, my darling, where are you? What are you dreaming about? Are you ever going to wake up?" But the child remained in a deep, deep sleep.

Gentle Spring came and sprinkled some magic in the air. Soon the first signs of tiny green shoots started to appear in the ground where the stone had been planted. The creatures of the garden were overjoyed. Each day they peeped at the shoots as they grew strong in the soil. Soon there were sprouting branches from the main stems and then they could see some little pink buds emerging from the branches.

'Oh, isn't it magical that the tree is growing so well in the earth. I awake each day and wonder what I'll see. Soon the buds will burst into wonderful blossoms," Betty said to Lady, as they buzzed and hopped from rose to rose.

"It won't be long until we see flowers and, as Wind foretold, the spell would finally be broken," Lady said.

Each day, the tree produced more and more branches, growing up taller and higher in the sky, wrapping around each other to reach the strong rays of the sun. The buds burst forth into the most beautiful soft pink blossoms, covering the tree like a veil of pink. The tree resembled a great big giant candy floss. The creatures were spellbound and stared at the magical wonder unfolding before them.

Finally, one day in the month of May, tiny peaches burst forth from the blossoms on the myriad of branches of the great tree. In the child's bedroom, Julia opened her eyes and gave a little yawn.

"Mama, where am I? I've had a lovely long dream," and she reached out and touched her mother's hand.

"Oh, darling, you're awake! I'm so, so happy!" her

mother cried, cradling the little girl to her.

Everybody in Ballinclea House roared with laughter and joy and cheered as the gardener rushed about the garden shouting, "She's awake, Julia's awake!" The flowers all nodded with happiness, and the creatures rushed about furiously with excitement. Betty hugged her pal, Lady.

"Oh, isn't it marvellous news! I can't wait to fly and rest on Julia's beautiful hair again," Betty said and flew off to explore some new plants that had arrived that day from the nursery.

A great change came over the once magnificent peach tree in the garden. It began to wither and die. In its place stood a shy speckled thrush, which hopped around for a few minutes and then flew away. The tiny creatures watched and wondered as the bird soared up and out of sight in the clear blue sky. All that remained of the once magnificent fruit tree was now only a tarred and gnarled piece of wood.

Julia recovered fully, and in a short while she played and ran again among the gardens of Ballinclea House. Connie wove a special silk web for the little girl, stretching from the leg of the table to the child's chair, where Julia took her herbal tea in the afternoon.

"Oh, my goodness. What a wonderful web! So perfect, and I can see all the colours of the rainbow. Thank you so much, little spider," said Julia, taking Connie up in her tiny frail hand and releasing her on a violet plant nearby.

People whispered about the garden and its peach tree. All kinds of rumours spread about how the beautiful child,

Julia, recovered. They believed that when the once magnificent peach tree died it carried off the illness which had struck down Julia. Others whispered that the shy thrush was the king's son.

Finally the curse over Ballinclea House was gone forever. The new tree was just as magnificent as the old one. Golden peaches hung from its boughs. The peaches were soft and perfumed with a heavenly taste. Each fruit dripped with succulent peach juice, and was covered in a sugar coated glaze, that shone and twinkled like frost, but melted once eaten in the mouth. The fruits left a most delicious aftertaste of wild honey and peach juice. No peach was ever bad, hard or too ripe; the magnificent tree only produced the most perfect of fruits. People came from far and wide to partake of these wondrous fruits without any harm.

Wind and the creatures of the garden alone knew what had taken place. They kept this secret in their little hearts forever, as they lived out the rest of their happy lives in the garden of Ballinclea.

Acknowledgements

I would like to thank Mr. William O'Brien for his kind and generous sponsorship, without which the book would never have got published.

I would also like to thank Ms. Dorothy Podmore, Vancouver, Canada for editing the stories. I would also like to thank Ms. Cassie Clarke for her wonderful illustration.

100% of the proceeds of the book will go to the Children's Medical Research Foundation, Crumlin

Lightning Source UK Ltd.
Milton Keynes UK
UKHW02f1238180418
321262UK00008B/62/P